Y0-EAA-209

SPECIAL MESSAGE TO READERS

This book is published under the auspices of
THE ULVERSCROFT FOUNDATION
(registered charity No. 264873 UK)

Established in 1972 to provide funds for research, diagnosis and treatment of eye diseases. Examples of contributions made are: —

A new Children's Assessment Unit at Moorfield's Hospital, London.

•

Twin operating theatres at the Western Ophthalmic Hospital, London.

•

A Chair of Ophthalmology at the University of Leicester.

•

The establishment of a Royal Australian College of Ophthalmologists "Fellowship".

You can help further the work of the Foundation by making a donation or leaving a legacy. Every contribution, no matter how small, is received with gratitude. Please write for details to:

**THE ULVERSCROFT FOUNDATION,
The Green, Bradgate Road, Anstey,
Leicester LE7 7FU, England.
Telephone: (0116) 236 4325**

**In Australia write to:
THE ULVERSCROFT FOUNDATION,
c/o The Royal Australian College of
Ophthalmologists,
27, Commonwealth Street, Sydney,
N.S.W. 2010.**

HELLER IN THE ROCKIES

Luke Heller's job — to handle security at a hotel in the Colorado Rockies — should have been a peaceful little assignment. But death was stalking the slopes — first in the shape of a grisly murder, then as a violent robbery. Almost before he knew it, the man from Tombstone was calling upon all his experience as a one-time Pinkerton detective and Confederate sharpshooter in order to catch the killers in a brutal, explosive finale.

*Books by David Whitehead
in the Linford Western Library:*

HELLER
STARPACKER
TRIAL BY FIRE

DAVID WHITEHEAD

HELLER IN THE ROCKIES

Complete and Unabridged

LINFORD
Leicester

First published in Great Britain in 1992 by
Robert Hale Limited
London

First Linford Edition
published 1996
by arrangement with
Robert Hale Limited
London

The right of David Whitehead to be identified
as the author of this work has been asserted
by him in accordance with the
Copyright, Designs and Patents Act, 1988

Copyright © 1992 by David Whitehead
All rights reserved

British Library CIP Data

Whitehead, David, *1958*–
 Heller in the Rockies.—Large print ed.—
 Linford western library
 1. English fiction—20th century
 2. Large type books
 I. Title
 823.9'14 [F]

ISBN 0–7089–7957–2

Published by
F. A. Thorpe (Publishing) Ltd.
Anstey, Leicestershire

Set by Words & Graphics Ltd.
Anstey, Leicestershire
Printed and bound in Great Britain by
T. J. Press (Padstow) Ltd., Padstow, Cornwall

This book is printed on acid-free paper

Dedicated to
Sharon, Lauran and Lane Hullar,
with special thanks to Link Hullar
for his contribution to this story.

1

JESSE JAMES never should have done it.

It wasn't enough that he and his brother Frank had killed and robbed and generally raised Ned right across the Midwest: that his bank robbery in Savannah, Missouri, had left a father and son dead in the dust; that his derailing of a Chicago & Rock Island express back in '73 had resulted in the engineer being scalded to death; or that he'd relieved a Kansas City fairground of more than ten thousand dollars in a job that took barely as many minutes to perform.

No, that wasn't nearly enough for the squint-eyed sonofabitch. He'd also gone and killed three Pinkerton detectives in less than one month, and in the eyes of Allan Pinkerton himself that made it three outrages too many.

So the crusty old Scotsman had resolved to nail Jesse good and nail him *quick*.

And now, on the freezing cold night of January 25th 1875, the men of Pinkerton's National Detective Agency looked almost certain to have Frank and Jesse James within their grasp. At last.

Following a sighting of the brothers around the home of Zerelda and Reuben Samuels (their mother and step-father), undercover Pinkerton operative Jack Ladd, who'd been 'working' at the Askew place just across the road, had received word that the boys were intending to 'visit the old lady' for a while.

At once more secret wheels had been set in motion. More operatives were dispatched to Liberty, Missouri, and a base of operations established at the north end of town. The local sheriff was also brought in on the operation, as was the secret committee of townsmen who'd grown sick and tired of Jesse's homicidal shenanigans.

During the fourth week of the New Year, a coded message came through that Jesse and Frank had been seen entering the family home. William Pinkerton, commanding the operation from a base in Kansas City, decided to spring his trap at ten o'clock that same night.

A furtive train journey had taken the posse through Clay County, and by the appointed hour the Samuels' farm, in darkness now but painted silver by the swollen moon above, was completely surrounded.

"Are they sure he's still in there?" asked one whispered voice of his companion.

"About as sure as they're likely to be. Ladd heard that Jesse's plannin' to stick around for a fortnight at least."

A rustling of brush caused the two operatives to turn just as a third hunched figure emerged from the bushes fringing the western perimeter. Moonlight spilled off the barrels of their guns.

"Don't shoot!" hissed a familiar voice. "It's only me!"

As the two Pinkertons allowed themselves to relax again, the newcomer's eyes settled briefly on the one-storey farmhouse rising up sixty yards ahead of them, plank-built and mean in the moonlight. "I'spect you'll be getting plenty of other targets to shoot at before tonight grows much older."

"I 'spect," the first voice agreed, vapour steaming from between its owner's whiskery lips.

He and his companion waited for the third man to scrabble up alongside them. This took a while, because the third man was cradling a strange-looking lamp with a hemispherical, cast-iron base and a brass top from which protruded two wicks. It was a potflare, what some called 'Grecian fire', and the idea was that this man would go on ahead, force open one of the farmhouse's shuttered windows and toss the lamp inside. The heavy metal base would ensure that it landed right-side up, and its turpentine contents, feeding the wicks, would act like a flare, illuminating the now-shadowy interior for the rest of the posse to see.

Gradually word filtered along the line of men encircling the house. In silence they began a slow, careful approach, bellies to the earth, inching forward on elbows, all of them sliding across the near-frozen ground like giant snakes in the darkness.

★ ★ ★

Right through that day, small pockets of Liberty committee-men had started congregating just beyond the stand of oaks that formed a natural barrier a quarter-mile back from the Samuels' place. When the last of the Pinkertons had arrived and the whole bunch had moved out, the copse in which they'd held their last, hurried rehearsal had fallen quiet and deserted, save for the odd stamp or whinny from the townsmens' tethered horses. Two men had been left behind to keep an eye on things, a local man named Hopkins and a seasoned Pinkerton operative by the name of Luke Heller.

It was Heller, quieting the string of restless animals with nonsense words, who first caught the sounds of another horse coming from the northeast, being driven hard through the timber. A split second later the townsman heard it as well, and began to ask, "What — ?"

Heller crossed the moon-silvered glade like a wraith, silencing him with a raised left hand while his right dipped towards the Colt in the shoulder-rig beneath his greatcoat.

The thrubbing of the horse's hooves was growing rapidly louder, so close now that he could catch the small jingling sounds of bit and buckle as well. During the War he'd been one of Colonel John Bell Hood's 'Hardeman Rifles', and now his lively green marksman's eyes caught a flash of movement a little way off to the left.

He turned in that direction but stared hard to one side of it, knowing that he'd pick out more details that way rather than by staring directly at it.

A quarter-minute later he saw horse and rider both heading towards the copse at break-neck speed, with the moon-thrown shadows of the bare branches above racing backwards off the rider's hat and shoulders as he weaved the horse between and around the tall, thick-boled trees.

Within another pair of seconds the horse came thundering into the clearing with the rider straightening his legs in the stirrups and hauling back on the reins. The animal skidded to a halt, tearing up clods of loamy soil and scattering crisp dead leaves in a brown shower. Heller came over with his Colt in hand; he saw foam around the horse's mouth and lather on its flanks.

The rider pretty-near fell out of the saddle. His voice was low and raspy and he was breathing hard. "Luke, is that you? Hold your fire, for God's sake!"

Heller came closer with the townsman right behind him. He couldn't see the newcomer's face for the shadow cast by his hat-brim, but he knew the voice; it belonged to Wes Calder, one of the Pinkerton men who'd been left back at their headquarters in Liberty.

"Wes! What the — ?"

Calder cut in; "Have they gone in yet, Luke? Our men?"

"About twenty minutes ago."

Calder swore. "We've got to stop them!"

"*What?*"

"The James boys . . . they're not up at the Samuels' place! We just got word . . . they were sighted in Laurinsport this afternoon!"

Laurinsport? That was fifty, sixty miles to the south. "You're sure?"

"Sure enough to've risked my neck ridin' hell for leather out here to stop the attack."

Heller wasn't sure but he thought

later that he'd muttered an oath. At the time he was too busy considering the implications of this new turn of events. Dammit, the Pinkertons didn't wage war on innocent folks, and if Jesse and Frank James really *were* someplace else, then the attack must be called off. Apart from which . . .

An unpleasant tingle washed across Heller's face. God alone knew how many of the posse might turn trigger-happy when Johnson's potflare lit up the Samuels house. He'd seen normally stable men go a little crazy before in such circumstances. And intelligence had it that there were three innocent adults in there, and four children.

He thought about how long the posse had been gone, how long it could take to position everyone before moving in. There was still a slim chance that the mission could be aborted if he moved swiftly enough . . .

Shoving his handgun back into leather, he hustled across to the string of horses and untied the reins of the first animal in line. It was a thick-limbed town horse, not an ideal choice, but he didn't have time to be choosy. With Wes and the townsman watching him, he tightened the girth by touch and powered up into the saddle. Wheeling the animal around, he heeled it in the ribs and took off into the darkness, heading for the Samuels place a quarter-mile away.

The horse was an ungainly mover, not used to shifting itself with any degree of speed or urgency. The ride was helter-skelter and jarring. As trees flashed past to either side of him, Heller felt as if his teeth were being shaken loose.

For a time all he knew was the crackle and thud of the horse's hooves crushing the dead leaves beneath them, the ice-cold air whipping past his face, a blurred, nightmare kaleidoscope of dark, sturdy tree-trunks looming directly in his path, only to lurch to one side or the other at the last moment.

Again he thought about the possible consequences of the raid. Had they been at 'Castle James', as the Samuels place had been christened by the Pinkertons, Jesse and Frank might have given themselves up without a fight in order to spare their mother any further grief. If they did not surrender within moments of the attack being launched, the posse could only draw one conclusion; that the boys were planning to fight or run. And in that kind of situation, where the tension was so thick you'd need a bread-knife to cut it, even the best of men tended to shoot first and ask questions later.

Three innocent adults, he thought. *And four children* . . .

It was about then that the thick-limbed horse stumbled on a tree-root and went crashing down on its forelegs, ploughing a great, ugly scar out of the ground and cutting the air with a shrill, panicky scream.

Heller yelled out himself at the surprise of it, kicked free of the stirrups and hit the ground running. Balance deserted him and he fell forward, rolled, came up with his greatcoat covered in mud and leaves and kept going through the night-time forest, chilled air sawing in and out of raw lungs as, behind him, the spooked horse quickly regained its feet.

The oaks began to thin and give way to patchy brush. Just beyond the brush Heller saw the Samuels place nestled at the centre of a roughly square section of flat, scrubby earth. As sweat dribbled into his eyes, he thought for a moment that he was going to make it after all.

But then —

But then there came a bright flash from inside the farmhouse, and a violent explosion shattered the night.

★ ★ ★

Luke Heller came awake with a start and an anguished kind of moan, sweat pebbling his forehead and twisted sheets trapping him in a soft but insistent cottony grip. For a moment he lay there in the darkness, wondering just where in hell he was and why for the love of God he'd suddenly started dreaming about that awful episode from his past.

Practically every night for the last fortnight he'd gone back to that time, always hoping that the outcome would be different, that somehow he'd reach the Samuels place in time to halt the attack.

But he hadn't managed it in real life, and showed little sign of accomplishing it in his dreams, either. There was just no escaping the fact that the attempt to capture the James boys on that winter Sunday night had gone tragically wrong. The potflare had been hurled into the Samuels place and had lit up one entire room, as intended. But Dr Samuels had knocked the thing into the fireplace with his cane and it had exploded, showering the house with shrapnel.

Heller threw back the sheet and sat up, exhausted but reluctant to chance going back to sleep. Even now, six years later, he remembered the complete chaos which had followed the explosion, the yelling, the screaming, the crying, the sounds of Zerelda Samuels trying to restore order in a voice that was eerily calm.

It was only once order *had* been restored to the farm that he'd been able to see for himself the full horror of what had happened there. Dr Samuels and his coloured maid had both received slight injuries, as had three of the children. The fourth, Jesse's eight-year-old half-brother Archie, died with most of his guts pooling on the floor. And as for Mrs Samuels, still trying to give orders in that damnably calm voice . . . well, a lump of metal had scrambled up much of her right arm; later she'd have to have it amputated at the elbow.

Heller shuddered, but after a time his heart slowed its pounding and the sweat began to dry against his skin. The shifting of the narrow cot beneath him and the constant rattle and clank filtering in through the small curtained window reminded him that he should be concentrating less on the past and more on the present, for at the moment he was in a cramped sleeping berth aboard the train that was taking him ever deeper into the Colorado Rockies, and a new chapter in his life as a private detective.

It had started one week earlier with a telegram addressed to Heller at his run-down little office in Tombstone, Arizona. A wealthy British industrialist named John Colfax had built a luxury hotel up in the high country, and needed someone to bolster security for a couple of months whilst his permanent man was recovering from a bad case of septicaemia. In his search for the right candidate, Heller's name had surfaced more than once, most recently from the railroader Ranald Lawrence, whose kidnapped daughter Heller had rescued from a Tong-run brothel in San Francisco several months earlier.

Colfax' wire stressed that his resort catered to the rich and famous, who craved rest and recreation in the secluded wilderness whilst still enjoying all the comforts of a rather palatial home. The successful replacement, he said, would frequently be called upon to exercise tact, diplomacy, restraint and vigilance.

Luke believed he could cut it. The son of a druggist from Mount Vernon, Ohio, he had known only city life up to the age of twelve, at which time his father, who had never been a well man, suffered a severe stroke.

After that, things had only gone from bad to worse for his mother, for not only did she have to see to young Luke's welfare, but also tend a fully-grown man who was now just as helpless as a new-born babe. All this, Heller remembered, and spent ten hours a day boiling up and ironing out other folks' washing to make a living.

Yessir, they'd been dark days . . . And with finances growing steadily tighter,

Heller's mother had finally decided to accept her elder brother's offer to take the boy off her hands for a year or two, until she could get back on her feet.

Uncle Dick Coleman owned a cattle spread down around Sulphur Springs, Texas, nothing grand, but a living. The boy had not been looking forward to being packed off to Uncle Dick — whom he had never met — and had cried away the entire thousand-mile stage and train journey. But as it turned out, the eight years he eventually spent with his mother's brother were among the happiest he had ever known.

For there, among the rolling grasslands of East Texas, he had learned to ride and rope and brand and shoot. In the company of so many men he had grown up fast, enjoying his role in this rough, masculine world.

As he grew from boy into man, so he began to help drive his uncle's beef north to the markets in Wichita, K.C. and Topeka, fighting off rustlers and Comanches alike with a tenacity that surprised even himself. Admiring his spunk, his uncle grew to love him, and Luke to love Dick Coleman in return.

Then came the War, and the now sixteen-year-old promptly followed his uncle into the 4th Texas Volunteers, seeing service as one of 'A' Company's 'Hardeman Rifles'. He grew up faster than ever then, and became a damn' fine sharpshooter too.

At War's end four years later, he and his uncle returned to Sulphur Springs. There was much to be done in this time of Reconstruction. The north was starved of beef, and down south wild cattle were to be found roaming free among the *brasada*-lands.

But four weeks after his twenty-first birthday, Heller got word that his father had passed on, and realising that his duty in life was now to support his mother, he reluctantly left Texas to go back east.

At first he tried to follow in his father's footsteps and become a druggist, but he lacked the interest so vital when handling potentially-lethal medicaments. He got a job in a meat processing plant, had a fight and was fired. He worked as a dishwasher, then clerked for a while with a freight company. When this palled, he went after a bank-teller's position but didn't get it because he had no head for more complicated sums.

At the age of twenty-three and engaged to be married to a young lady who eventually ran off with a drummer from Saratoga, New York — he enrolled in the Urbana Police Department and won a commendation from Mayor Albert Lancaster himself when he foiled a bank robbery by judicious use of the night-stick. But when he tried the same trick again six months later he got himself shot in the left shoulder and posted to a desk job.

After that, police work was never the same; there were too damn' many reports to fill in and file for one thing. So he up and quit again, and went to work for Allan Pinkerton, and that kind of brought him back to the James business, and his recurring dream . . .

Now, in the hours before dawn, Luke Heller once again thought through those events which had shaped his life and brought him to this moment. Around him, the train climbed higher into the Rockies. It would be good to get out of Tombstone for a while, he concluded. He could use a break from the city, an opportunity to enjoy some good fresh air and clean wilderness living again.

And anyway, just how difficult could it be to ride herd on a hotel filled with the cream of society? Why, he might even get in a little hunting and fishing himself — and be paid handsomely for the pleasure, too.

After a while the detective stretched out on his shifting cot once again and allowed sleep to reclaim him while darkness still remained and the train rumbled higher into the mountains.

★ ★ ★

Early morning found Luke working through a plate of ham and eggs in the train's dining car. Dressed in a well-cut grey suit, white shirt and black string tie, the private detective with the short, neatly-combed black hair and square, moderately handsome face, looked more like a prosperous young banker at first glance. Closer observation, however, brought with it a hint of something more dangerous about the man's occupation, a hint validated by the Civilian model Frontier Colt resting comfortably in the shoulder-holster beneath his tailored jacket.

The gun was a beautiful weapon; as beautiful, that was, as any killing machine could ever be. It was short-barrelled, light and silver-plated, with cross-hatched walnut grips and impressive stopping-power. Out of habit, Luke had dropped spare loads into both coat pockets so that he was ready for any emergency, although it had to be said that he despised unnecessary gunplay.

As he finished his meal and started on his second cup of coffee, he turned his attention from his immediate surroundings to the rugged mountain view wheeling past beyond the long, low window to his right.

It was breathtaking. Stretch-barked aspens studded the incline, shelving steadily up and out of sight. Grass grew tall and lush, punctuated by a whole catalogue of colourful wild flowers. For a while the timber fell away to reveal a wide, mirror-still lake, then the timber shouldered back, pushing higher and higher up the slope.

Suddenly Luke sensed a change come over the dining car's other occupants, and turned his attention from the window to the head of the carriage to see what had caused such a stir among the many male passengers. A young Chinese woman had entered the car, turning heads as she made her way along the carpeted aisle between the tables.

She was beauty personified, no more than twenty or so, and her thin, delicate eyebrows arched appealingly above two clear, expressive almond eyes. Her small, pert nose was set above full, heart-shaped lips, and when she spotted Heller and smiled at him, she revealed teeth like pearls. Her midnight-black hair was simply cut in an attractive bob, and its sheen matched that coming off her silk jacket and pants. The rich green colour of her garments served to enhance the beauty of her olive complexion.

Heller stood up as she reached him and held out a chair for her. He felt the envy of the men around him quite palpably, and enjoyed it. "Morning, Mai. Sleep well?"

She nodded. "*Shi*. Yes. And you?"

"Oh, fair."

The waiter arrived and he ordered

breakfast for her. Circumstances had thrown them together during Luke's hunt for the men who'd kidnapped the Lawrence girl.[1] Prior to meeting up with the Tombstone detective, Mai Lin had led a difficult existence. In her youth she had known both hard labour and prostitution, but Luke had rescued her from all of that. Now, however, their relationship was at something of a cross-roads. In one respect they were simply partners. But in another way they were much, much more.

For her part, Mai was happy to accompany Luke on his latest assignment. It would be good to have some quiet time with her companion, surrounded by the grandeur of the Rocky Mountains. And perhaps, she thought, there might be time for more than mere friendship on this trip. After almost a year together, perhaps the time

---

[1] As told in *Heller*.

was finally right to consider romance.

"Excited?" he asked.

She nodded. "Very," she said quietly, still self-conscious when speaking in English. "But relieved, too. So much travelling . . . it has been very tiring."

"Just wait till you get to the Mountain View Hotel," he told her with a grin. "You'll get all the rest you're ever likely to need."

"And time?" she asked eagerly. "To spend together?"

His eyes held hers. "If there *isn't* time," he promised softly, "I'll *make* it."

It was too bad that neither of them could even begin to guess just how hectic the next few days were going to be; how hectic, and how violent.

2

ABOUT two hours later the conductor signalled the end of their journey with a bellowed, *"Grey Springs, next stop! Next stop Grey Springs!"*

The train had already begun to slow as Heller and Mai prepared to debark.

John Colfax had arranged to meet them here at the station house, and as Luke worked his way towards the front of the carriage, he saw a number of people milling around in front of the whitewashed structure, either waiting for passengers or freight shipments.

When at last the Baldwin squealed and shushed to a halt, Luke and Mai stepped down from the passenger car and started looking around for the Englishman. It was surprising how much chaos there was at such a minor stopover. Then, above all the noise of trains and travellers, the detective heard his name being called in a clear, unmistakably British accent.

"Heller? Mr Heller?"

The man approaching them was soft and pleasant in appearance. His expensively-tailored dark suit was complemented by a derby hat of matching hue and an ornate watch chain that spanned the front of his brocade vest. His face was that of a cherub, with deep blue eyes that revealed some of the determination that had made him a millionaire by the age of thirty-five and a considerably richer man in the decade which followed. The dapper little man came forward with his right hand extended, and was met by the smiling stranger who had come so highly recommended to him.

"You must be John Colfax," Luke greeted his new employer. "Pleased to meet you."

"A pleasure reciprocated, Mr Heller," the Englishman responded. "I am delighted to have you join us at the Mountain View Hotel. I trust you had a pleasant journey up from Tombstone?"

"Long and bumpy, Mr Colfax." Luke gestured to Mai and spoke again. "May I introduce my friend and associate, Mai Lin? You'll recall that I mentioned in my cable message that she'd be accompanying me.

"That is correct, Mr Heller," Colfax agreed. "Miss Lin. Welcome to our mountain paradise." His expression said something a little different, though, something Luke had seen a thousand times before; distaste and distrust of a foreigner.

If Mai also saw it, she gave no indication. With her tiny hands clasped across her flat stomach, she smiled and offered a slight bow from the waist. Her natural Oriental reserve had come into play now that a stranger was present. While she had learned to be open and intimate with Heller, she still maintained her distance in the presence of others.

Returning his attention to his new security man, Colfax lifted the silver-tipped cane in his left hand and pointed in the direction of a buckboard stalled about a block's distance away. A middle-aged man in nondescript western clothing sat in the driver's seat, apparently napping as he waited to return his employer and the newcomers to the mountain hotel. "Our transportation is just down the street. If you will direct the porter to load your bags, we'll be on our way . . . "

"Mai will see to the porter, Mr Colfax," Heller replied. "I have to get my horse from the stock car."

As he strode off towards the rear of the train, Luke wondered in what mood he would find the horse known as Goddam. At best the gelding was ornery, at worst downright mean. Many times the horse had attempted to throw, bite or otherwise maim his master. In fact, Luke often wondered just who the master really was in their uneasy relationship. On more than one occasion he had come close to unloading the animal on some unsuspecting buyer, but somehow had never been able to follow through. By now he knew the horse, bad moods and all, so he guessed he might just as well keep the mean-spirited varmint.

As he approached the car he saw a railroad worker stroking the horse's neck as the animal nuzzled the man's chest softly. It looked like the horse might be having a good day, Luke thought as he admired the mount's sleek, coffee-coloured coat. Coming up to the horse, he threw caution to the wind and reached out to scratch between its twitching ears, only to jerk his hand back quickly as the animal's big yellow teeth snapped at him.

"*Goddam!*" Heller exclaimed.

The horse broke wind then, almost in greeting.

"I don't think he likes you, mister," the railroad worker opined as Luke handed the man his claim ticket and took the horse by the reins.

"I *know* he doesn't like me," he replied, leading the horse towards the buckboard, where Colfax and Mai were already seated with the baggage — including Luke's big, forty-pound Denver saddle — loaded in the back. Heller tied Goddam to the rear of the wagon and climbed aboard for the final leg of the trip.

"The journey out to the hotel should take about half an hour," Colfax informed them. "But it is a truly beautiful excursion."

Colfax wasn't kidding. The mountains were rugged and majestic, with towering peaks and deep, verdant valleys. At times the trail they were following would disappear into sizeable thickets of timber from which little was visible other than the forest that surrounded them. The Mountain View Hotel might only be thirty minutes from Grey Springs, but there was no doubting the absolute seclusion it offered.

After riding in silence for a short time, Heller turned the conversation towards his duties at the hotel. "Just what *are* my responsibilities where security is concerned, Mr Colfax?"

The Englishman waved one hand airily. Sunlight spilled off the gold rings on his fingers. "You and your opposite number will be working on a shift system, Mr Heller. Eight hours on, eight hours off. In that way we can guarantee to have someone available at all times. Not that I anticipate too many problems. The majority of your work will involve the gentle care and handling of wealthy patrons who have, perhaps, had a little too much to drink. Quite mundane work for you, I'm certain."

"I can use a little quiet boredom in my life," Heller muttered drily, and Mai Lin nodded in agreement. "You mentioned my 'opposite number', Mr Colfax. Who will that be, exactly?"

"Oh, chap named Jim Nodeen. Perhaps you've heard of him?"

Heller nodded. "If it's Jim Nodeen the pugilist you're referring to."

"It is."

Nodeen had once been a big name in the prize-fighting game, a good heavyweight who'd never quite made it to the title. But that had been quite some time ago, and as his career had taken a dive, so he'd dropped out of public life.

They continued rolling along the wooded trail. A rabbit darted across the clearing in front of them, and Heller saw sign of other game among the trees that lined the pathway. When the clear high country air began to tremble with gunfire ten minutes later the Frontier Colt appeared in his hand as if by magic, but to his surprise, Colfax' only reaction was a hearty chuckle.

"It's all right, Mr Heller! Listen . . . that is merely some of the guests enjoying our excellent hunting facilities, sir, not one of the gunfights of which you westerners are so fond!"

Luke slipped the Colt back into leather, feeling just a little foolish. Colfax, however, seemed impressed by his quick reactions. "I can see that Ranald Lawrence did not exaggerate your prowess, sir."

"Or my enthusiasm," Luke agreed sheepishly.

The Englishman glanced around the mountain paradise. "The hotel is filled to capacity at the moment," he explained, "with a waiting list for reservations. It seems that we have become quite the fashionable resort for the holiday season. Lawyers, bankers and businessmen have flooded here for a little taste of the 'wild' west. At the Mountain View they can enjoy all the pleasures of these glorious surroundings without forsaking any of life's little luxuries. But there is no need for further explanation, for I see we're almost there."

As the buckboard turned a corner in the crude trail, Luke got his first look at the magnificent turreted structure which had been carefully constructed to fit perfectly among the trees and mountains. Painted a spotless white, the three-storey stone building included all the 'gingerbread' decorations presently so popular. It was obvious to the man from Tombstone that no expense had been spared on the hotel's exterior and grounds. Stained glass windows and intricate woodwork gave the resort an aristocratic air, with meticulous landscaping and gardens providing the finishing touches that made the Mountain View Hotel the high country Utopia that John Colfax had described.

As they continued their approach, stables and utility buildings could be seen at the rear of the hotel. The detective whistled lightly under his breath as the wagon came to a stop before the front entrance and doormen hurried forward to assist the passengers.

Colfax was in charge of things at once, speaking with the calm authority of a man who is accustomed to having his orders obeyed without question. "Howard, take Mr Heller's luggage up to three-oh-three. The, ah, lady, will be staying in three-oh-four. Chuck, please see that Mr Heller's horse is taken around to the stables and given every care."

Luke didn't miss the disparaging way Colfax had referred to Mai, and as they climbed down from the buckboard he put one hand gently on the dapper little man's left arm. "I think we'd do well to get one thing straight before we go any further, Mr Colfax," he said quietly.

The Englishman looked up at him, blue eyes innocuous. "Mr Heller?" he asked questioningly.

"That 'lady' you just referred to," Luke explained, still keeping it quiet. "She really is a lady, Mr Colfax. One of the best."

Colour crept into the smaller man's smooth cheeks. "I — "

"Sure, she's a foreigner," Luke cut in. "But over here, so are *you*."

He took his hand away from the Englishman's arm and said, "Now, if you don't think it's such a good idea to employ me after all . . . "

Colfax looked up at him for a moment before shaking his head. "No, Mr Heller. I . . . I stand corrected. We British are sometimes inclined towards imperialism. Forgive me if I caused offence." He brushed past the taller man and extended one hand to Mai. "Here, my dear; allow me to help you down from there."

When Colfax was through playing the gentleman, he led them up the wide stone steps towards the tall double doors which stood open in greeting. A large veranda ran along the front of the building, where scattered guests sat in conversation as white-coated waiters glided from table to table with drinks-laden trays held at head-height.

Entering the lobby, Luke and Mai were momentarily stunned by the ornate beauty of the hotel's interior. Cut-glass chandeliers hung from a high, vaulted ceiling. Stained wood panelling, silk wallpaper and thick, scarlet carpet gave the reception area an atmosphere of affluence. Bellboys were already carrying their luggage up the wide stairway while Luke and his companion stood in awe of their luxurious surroundings.

Colfax smiled at their obvious sense of wonder. "Welcome to the Mountain View Hotel," he said, and this time he really sounded like he meant it. "Obviously you're standing in our lobby right now," he went on. "The establishment has forty guest rooms located on the first and second floors. The ground floor consists of the lobby, restaurant, bar and gaming room. My offices are also located down here, just along that corridor to the right. We employ more than thirty members of staff on a regular basis, including maids, waiters, cooks, guides and hunters, and generally we cater for between seventy or eighty guests at any one time. As you will soon see for yourselves, our facilities and services are second to none. Our guests want for nothing."

Colfax paused as he spotted a man

heading their way from the other side of the lobby. He was a big fellow, some two hundred and fifty pounds in weight and several inches over six feet in height. His frame was obviously powerful but in decline, with a stomach that stretched at the buttons of his fancy vest and a face that showed the effects of years in the ring. His ears were crumpled to the sides of his head and a nose that had lost all recognisable shape long ago sat like a big, ugly wart in the centre of his face. He smiled as he approached his employer — at least Luke guessed it was meant to be a smile — and the gesture revealed mis-shapen yellow teeth set into pink, saliva-shiny gums.

As he lumbered up, running a hand through the fine, downy grey hair that stippled his scalp, he said, "Howdy, Mr Colfax. Saw you come in, thought I'd just step across an' let you know everythin's runnin' jake."

"Good." The hotel-owner turned to indicate Luke and Mai. "Allow me to make some introductions, Jim, this is your new partner, Lucas Heller from down in Arizona, and Mr Heller's lady-friend, Mai Lin." He caught Luke's eye as he said 'lady-friend', and Luke was pleased to hear that there was no disdain in the way he said it this time. "Mr Heller — allow me to present Jim Nodeen. I hope the pair of you will enjoy a long and successful association."

"Sure, Mr Colfax," Nodeen said in his slow, gravelly voice, cracking another smile at the Englishman. "You know you can count on me. Howdy, Heller. Heard of you, boy."

Luke looked into Nodeen's piggy little eyes. They looked red and sore, older than their forty years, a drinker's eyes unless he was much mistaken. There was also the faintest aroma of alcohol coming off his breath as he spoke. A big, successful prizefighter gone to seed, Luke decided. And leery as hell of anyone new coming in who might somehow usurp his present position of power.

Against his better judgement, Luke took the paw Nodeen offered, and was not at all surprised when the former pugilist put more pressure into his grip than was necessary.

Then the towering brute turned his gaze onto Mai Lin, and something else entered his eyes, a faint, animal gleam of lust. The one-time prizefighter all but drooled as his imagination quickly stripped Mai bare. He spoke not a word, but his desire was obvious, and Mai gave a shudder as she met his leering gaze.

Colfax sensed her unease and broke the moment with a few brisk words. "Jim, be so kind as to show Mr Heller and Miss Lin to their rooms, would you? You might also care to explain your duties to, ah, Lucas, is it?"

"Luke."

"Capital. Now, if you will excuse me, I have work to do, but I look forward to seeing you both later this evening."

As Colfax began walking down the

carpeted hallway towards his office, the ex-pugilist growled, "All right — follow me!"

Nodeen hurried up the stairs on long, thick legs. Luke and Mai had to hustle to keep up with him. As they started down the third floor hallway, the giant glanced over one brawny shoulder and said to Luke, "Does she speak English, the Celestial?"

The derogatory term brought a sudden surge of temper which Luke had to fight to keep down. "Why don't you ask her?" he suggested coolly.

Nodeen came to an abrupt halt, turned and did just that. "Speakee English, little darlin'?"

Very slowly Mai inclined her head.

"Good. 'Cause this room here, it's three-oh-four. Yours. For you. Savvy?" Mai nodded again, and he smiled down at her in what he thought to be his most gallant fashion, only managing to expose his cracked teeth whilst expelling a gust of foul breath.

Mai glanced up at Luke, clearly

uncomfortable around the prizefighter, and he gave her a nod of encouragement. As she let herself through the door and into the room, Nodeen gestured across the hall at 303.

"That's yours, buddy."

The big man waited until Luke had turned the doorknob and let himself inside before adding quietly, "Oh, an' Heller. Just so's we understand each other. This 'association' business that Colfax was bleatin' on about just now. I wouldn't want you to run away with the notion that it was gonna be an equal partnership. I got seniority around here, you got that? That means we do things *my* way."

Luke looked into the other man's lumpy red face. "Colfax didn't bring me in here to be your assistant, Nodeen," he replied evenly. "Oh, I'll listen to what you have to say, sure. Like you said, you've been around here longer than me. But at the end of the day, I don't care whether we do the job your way or mine; just so long as we do it the *best* way."

Nodeen only grunted.

"And one other thing," Luke added with a cool smile. "It is just as well that we understand each other. So I'm telling you this now; keep those beady little eyes in your face and a civil tongue in your punch-drunk head when you speak to the lady. You got *that*? And while you're at it, you might go easy on the booze."

Nodeen opened his mouth to roar something indignant, but Luke was already sick and tired of him. In disgust he slammed the door shut in his new partner's face.

3

ONE hour later Luke left his room and went across to knock on Mai's door. A moment later he heard her small, child's voice coming from the other side of the panels. "Who is there?"

"It's me."

The door opened straightaway and she peered seriously up into his face. It was obvious that she had taken a very serious dislike to Jim Nodeen, but what the hell, that made two of them.

"You want to go downstairs and take a look around?" he asked.

She shook her head, sending a shiver through her black hair. "No, thank you, Luke."

"Sure?"

"I would like to rest until dinner, if you don't mind. The journey has left me . . . " she frowned, trying to think of the right word, " . . . fatigued."

"All right. But . . . " He reached down to lift her oval face a little. "Don't worry yourself. About Nodeen, I mean. He's all bluster. Forget him and enjoy yourself for the next few weeks."

She gave a delicate shrug. "Very well." She didn't sound all that enthusiastic, though, and although he smiled down at her, she made no attempt to return the expression.

He descended the stairs quickly. In the hour since their arrival, he had unpacked his travelling bag and cleaned up with the cool, refreshing water provided in the pitcher on top of the washstand in his room. After a change of shirts, he was now ready to see the sights of the Mountain View Hotel. Colfax had mentioned no special timetable to which he should adhere, so he figured first to familiarise himself with the layout of the place, and then go find Nodeen and attempt to get a handle on the exact nature of his duties.

He had no sooner stepped off the final stair and started across the lobby than a bellboy approached him, asking around a wide smile, "Show you around, Mr Heller?"

Luke pulled up short. The boy was about seventeen years old, with short sandy hair just visible beneath his red pill-box hat, and ambitious blue eyes. He wore a short red jacket with sharp creases and brass buttons, and black pants with a wide yellow stripe running down each outer seam. The high country sun had brought out a rash of freckles across his small nose.

"The name is Jess Monroe, sir," the bellboy went on. "And I'd sure be happy to give you a tour of the facilities."

Luke returned his smile. "Pleased to meet you, Jesse," he replied. "This place sure is something. I think I'd appreciate having someone show me around."

"Well, you've already seen the lobby," the youngster said, taking charge at once. Pointing down the corridor along which John Colfax had disappeared earlier he continued, "That's where you'll usually find Mr Colfax, should you need to see him at any time. He's got private living quarters down there, too. I suppose it might be of some interest to the new security man to know that the hotel safe is kept in Mr Colfax' office?"

Luke's smile broadened. News travelled fast in this place; he'd remember that. "Yes, I guess it would," he agreed. "All right, mister. Lead on."

They crossed the spacious lobby side by side and passed through double doors on the far side which led into the bar, which was almost deserted at this time of the afternoon. Dark and quiet, with luxurious carpets and wood-panelled walls, the bar-room also featured an impressive display of original artworks and numerous coloured-glass mirrors.

"Like it?" Jesse asked casually.

"Well, let's just say that it's a far cry from the Oriental Saloon back in Tombstone," Luke replied. "I feel lucky when they spread clean sawdust on the floor there."

"Mr Colfax believes in the finest of everything," the bellboy said proudly. "And the folks that come here expect it."

Passing through the doors on the other side of the room, they entered the casino, where Heller stood amazed at all the various games of chance that lay before him. "I'll be damned!"

"You will if you waste your wages in here," the youth replied with a mischievous grin.

At once Luke's square face hardened. "Are you telling me that these games are rigged?" he asked softly, so's not to spook the room's other occupants.

The bellboy matched his tone. "Oh no, Mr Heller, nothing like that. Mr Colfax runs an honest casino, you can rely on that for sure. Believe me, that Limey makes enough off these guests in room, food and drinks to keep the casino running honest even if the players get lucky. But everyone knows the casino's the winner in these games. If the patrons won, it wouldn't be gambling, would it? But you've no need to concern yourself. This place might be expensive, but it's honest."

Luke nodded and surveyed the room again. As with the bar, it was largely quiet at the moment, but over by one of the long, curtained windows he saw Jim Nodeen glaring at him. The big man was sipping from a tumbler as he scowled at the pair of them. Luke only offered him a smile and a wink.

"Afternoon, Jimmy," he called casually.

Nodeen muttered a few choice words into his glass. No doubt he would have said more, and made it more vocal, had there not been a few gamblers present in the room.

As Luke and the bell-hop quit the

casino, young Jess said in an undertone, "You be careful there, Mr Heller. That's one dangerous man. Had a problem in here one night with an unruly drunk. Feller got right abusive, he did, then tried to swing a punch at Mr Nodeen."

"Oh? And what did Mr Nodeen do about that?"

"Darn' near beat him to death with his fists before Mr Colfax showed up." The boy's voice dropped even lower. "He drinks pretty heavily himself, you know."

"I kind of guessed that."

Breaking into a smile again, Jess ushered him back through the lobby and into the restaurant, which was located directly opposite. "Pretty fancy, huh?" the boy asked with obvious pride.

It was. The dining room was every bit as elegant as the rest of the hotel. In fact, Luke thought it was probably the finest room he had seen in his entire life. Plush carpets and linen tablecloths made up the foundation of the luxury present, but finer touches included elaborate silver candelabra and fresh flowers on each of the forty-odd tables. Again, original oil paintings in gilded frames decorated the walls, and Luke couldn't help but wonder at the price tag attached to this incredible structure and its furnishings.

"'Course," Jesse Monroe cut in, "staff take their meals out back, near the kitchens."

Luke nodded. "Thanks, Jess. It's been a real interesting tour." He handed the boy a quarter.

"You don't want me to show you around anyplace else?"

"No. I figure I've got my bearings straight now. Think I'll take a little wander on my lonesome." In truth he thought he might just as well go back to the casino and see if he couldn't get Nodeen to give him a little background on the hotel and the nature of the problems he was likely to encounter.

When they split up, he went back

across the lobby. Smartly-dressed clerks made themselves busy behind the mahogany registration desk, whilst a young girl in a black dress and white apron watered and dusted the many potted plants that gave added colour to the large room. He half-expected to find Nodeen in the bar, ordering a refill for his whiskey glass, but there was no sign of the other security man. Neither was he to be found in the casino, where he had been just minutes before.

With a shrug, the man from Tombstone turned on his heel and returned to the lobby, from whence he headed outside to stand for a moment on the cool, sunlight-dappled veranda. Deciding to go for a stroll in the gardens, he was soon impressed by the beauty of the plants and flowers, as well as the care and maintenance given to the extensive grounds. Only a year or so ago, this area had been wilderness, and the detective knew that just beyond these cultured grounds the forest remained wild and untamed. He listened for a while to the distant sounds of gunfire signalling the position of those guests enjoying some of the resort's superb hunting facilities, then continued on.

His walk took him around back of the hotel, where he again spotted the stables and decided on impulse to check on Goddam. "Afternoon," he greeted the stablehand as he entered. "The name's Heller. Security. How's that gelding of mine getting along?"

The liveryman approached with his hand outstretched. "That's one fine animal you got there, Mr Heller. Gentle as a lamb. He's just down the way there, third stall on your right."

Luke uttered a bewildered thanks as he followed the other man's directions. Just what was it that others saw in that horse, he wondered as he reached the animal and muttered a greeting. Goddam's only response was a loud fart as he continued to munch at the oats placed in the trough before him.

Luke shook his head. "Goddam," he

told the horse, "you are just about the most worthless nag I've ever owned. Jeez . . . about the smelliest, too."

The horse pointedly ignored him.

As Luke left the stable, he ran straight into an elderly gentleman in a dark grey suit. At once he reached out to stop the old-timer from losing his balance. "Uh . . . excuse me. I should have watched where I was going."

When the old man made no reply, Luke studied him a little closer. The fellow was seventy years old if he was a day, but his sunken blue eyes still held the determination of a much younger man. Fine white hair was plastered across his skull, and bushy side-whiskers framed his face. His expensive clothing clung to a lean, tall frame.

"Sir?"

The old man stood there, so preoccupied that he was hardly aware of Luke's presence.

"Are you all right, sir?"

At last the old man blinked a few

times, apparently returning to his senses at last. "What? Oh, yes, yes, I'm fine, thank you. But I seem to have lost my wife out here somewhere. You couldn't help me look for her, I suppose?"

"Of course. Finding people is one of my duties, sir. I'm the house detective, Luke Heller."

The old man swallowed dryly. "Obliged to you, Mr Heller. I'm Cameron, by the way, Austin Cameron from New York State. My wife's name is Juliet."

Although he appeared to be a take-charge fellow, Austin Cameron looked worn to a frazzle right now. In fact, he looked downright ill. Quickly Luke decided that his best course of action would be to return the old man to the hotel before setting out in search of his missing wife. After seeing him safely back to the lobby, he returned to the veranda, where he stood with his hands on his hips and ran his narrowed eyes across the landscape before him.

"Looking for someone?"

The voice drew his attention back to his immediate surroundings, and the attractive woman seated at a table eight feet away, regarding him over the lip of her expensive lead crystal glass.

She was one of the most beautiful women upon whom he had ever set eyes. A long, frilly silk dress encased her frame but did little to hide the ample curves it contained. Her peaches-and-cream complexion was enhanced by the skilled application of expensive beauty aids, and luxuriant blonde hair was curled and combed to frame a small, delicate face. Deep blue eyes, high cheekbones, a small, snubbed nose and full, inviting red lips completed the vision before him. As he came closer, the fragrance of her perfume washed over him. He had to clear his throat before attempting a response.

"I'm trying to help one of the guests find his wife. They were walking in the grounds and got separated."

"You're on the staff?"

"Yes'm." He introduced himself and named his position.

The woman — who was around thirty years of age — eyed him with open curiosity. "Ah. I wondered why you were wearing a revolver beneath your jacket," she said coolly. "I saw it just now, when you had your fists on your hips." She took another sip at her drink. "Does she have a name, this lost woman? Perhaps I've seen her around."

"Juliet Cameron," Luke supplied. "I don't have a description, but her husband's a frail-looking old gentleman with grey mutton-chop side-whiskers. Ring any bells?"

"Yes," she said with a nod and another cool smile. "I know the man very well. He's my husband."

Luke's surprise showed itself before he could mask it.

"You were expecting someone older?" she asked frankly.

"Well . . . uh . . . "

"Please, Mr Heller, won't you come

and join me for a moment? It's awfully tiresome having to stare up at you all the time, you know."

Luke was tempted. *Mighty* tempted. There was something about this woman, something animal, sensual and predatory, that made a man crave even a moment of her company. But somehow his sense of duty prevailed. "Uh . . . Mrs Cameron . . . Please don't think I'm speaking out of turn, but well, I think you ought to go find your husband and let him know that you're all right. He was pretty concerned to have lost you and . . . well, maybe I *am* speaking out of turn . . . "

Her eyes flashed. "I like a man who speaks his mind."

"Well, he didn't appear to be in the best of health. I think he might need you."

"Austin is much stronger than he looks," she pointed out with a remarkable lack of concern. "But tell me, Mr Heller . . . do you have anyone who needs *you*?"

The question made him think of Mai, and thinking of Mai helped break the spell she was weaving around him. "Yes'm," he said quietly.

She seemed to lose interest in him quite abruptly then, and become all business. Setting her glass aside, she stood up with a rustle of silk and inclined her head, her expression still bold but just a little frosty now. "Thank you for your concern about my husband's welfare," she purred formally. "Perhaps our paths will cross again."

He nodded. "Perhaps."

As he watched her walk away, Luke knew that he would have to watch that lady or run the risk of becoming another of her many victims. As far as he was concerned, her beauty made her all the more dangerous, and he was suddenly glad that Mai was along on this job, not only to keep him company, but also to keep him in line.

* * *

After a passable evening meal with some of the other hotel staff, Luke left Mai in the company of a few off-duty maids and went to keep a rendezvous with John Colfax and Jim Nodeen in the bustling lobby. The hotel appeared even more beautiful by candle- and lamp-light than it had during the day. Now, the place was positively vibrant.

"Some new guests have joined us this evening," Colfax explained in a confidential tone. "*Important* guests." He gestured discreetly towards the restaurant. "You see that grey-bearded fellow seated just inside the doorway there? That's Senator Parkinson from Ohio, here with his wife and some friends. That's Congressman and Mrs Jonathan MacBride from West Virginia sitting next to them, and the New York banker Noah Berry and, ah, associate." The 'associate' was a red-headed woman whose well-developed chest threatened to spill over the top of her low-cut gown every time she leaned forward.

"Very impressive, Mr Colfax," Nodeen mumbled, eyeing the woman's cleavage.

Luke, however, was more interested in someone else, a little weasel of a man seated in the far corner of the opulent room. He was a small man in ill-fitting clothing, and his face had a rodent-like quality that was almost inescapable. Shaggy brown hair topped the visage, worn long enough to touch his celluloid collar at the back.

"Excuse me, Mr Colfax, but do you happen to know the man occupying that corner table?"

Colfax narrowed his blue eyes. After a moment he shook his head. "I'm sorry, I don't think I do. But I can't be expected to keep track of each individual guest, you know. Why?"

Luke looked grim. "Because I believe it's Barney Phipps."

The hotel-owner frowned. "Oh? And just who is Barney Phipps, pray tell?"

"I sent him to jail about seven years ago, when I was working with the Pinkertons. Back then he was one of the best safe-crackers in the business."

Jim Nodeen snorted. "Aw, you're jumpin' at shadows, Heller. I've spoken with that feller. He's jake. Can't recall his name, but I remember he said he was in engineerin'. Spoke real educated, too."

"It's amazing what you can pick up in prison."

Colfax said, "Mr Heller, if you have proof that this man is who you say he is, we must act upon it at once. If you don't, I will not have him defamed. He is a guest, after all."

"Don't pay him no mind, Mr Colfax," Nodeen chimed in with a sneer in Heller's direction. "He's just tryin' to show off. I've got everythin' under control around here, and believe me, if that man's a safe-cracker, I'm a laundry girl."

Luke told him, "No starch in my collars, Jimmy." Then he sobered. "I'm serious, Mr Colfax. We'd better keep an eye on that feller. All right; maybe he *is* an engineer. But if he *isn't*, if he really *is* Barney Phipps, we'd better figure out exactly what he's up to here."

The Englishman considered for a moment. "All right. If you really think it necessary, then do what you must. But I'll expect you to be discreet." Colfax reached up to tug at his lapels. "Now, if you'll excuse me, I have work to do."

The Englishman left them to it. Luke watched him stroll away, then said, "Come on, Nodeen; we've got some work of our own to get on with."

The ex-pugilist bristled, straightening from an ape-like slouch to his full, imposing six feet plus. "I told you earlier, Heller; *I* run this show." But he lumbered off towards the casino while Luke went to check out the bar-room.

The evening passed uneventfully except for a small disturbance in the casino. Two gentlemen in their sixties who'd had a bit too much to drink began an argument over the roulette wheel. Fortunately, Luke managed to intervene before the violent-tempered Nodeen could arrive on the scene and possibly make the matter worse. With a firm hand upon each, he ushered the two men outside for a breath of fresh air, after which each sheepishly exchanged apologies and agreed to turn in for the evening.

Afterwards, Luke began to search for the man he believed to be Barney Phipps. It worried him that a known felon might be staying at the hotel, and he was anxious to confirm the identity of the weasel-faced man one way or the other. After thirty fruitless minutes, his uneasiness over failing to locate his quarry made him decide to check in on Colfax — and the hotel safe.

No sooner had he started down the hallway towards the Englishman's private offices than he caught a movement down at the far end of the corridor, where the shadows were at their thickest. A moment later he also heard part of a muffled, one-sided conversation.

" ... time for us to get better acquainted ... "

He recognised the voice almost at once. There was something familiar about the smaller of the two figures down there, too ...

As Luke hurried closer and his eyes became accustomed to the gloom, his fears were partially confirmed. As he'd suspected, the big fellow doing all the talking was Jim Nodeen. But the smaller form he was blocking into a darkened niche was not Mai, as he'd first thought, although in size and shape the girl was very similar; it was the pretty but now thoroughly intimidated young maid who'd been tending the plants in the lobby earlier that afternoon.

"Just what the hell's going on here?"

Luke didn't really need an answer. He saw all he needed to in the girl's bloodless face, the tears in her eyes, the quivering of her bottom lip, the way her arms were crossed protectively over her breasts.

Nodeen spun around, surprise in his eyes. "What . . . ?"

That was as far as he got before Luke landed a solid right cross to his jaw and sent him sprawling to the plush carpet. As Nodeen climbed slowly back to his feet, anger replaced surprise in his sore-looking eyes. "Damn you, Heller! I'll pay you for that!"

Luke put himself between the ex-prizefighter and the girl. "Like hell you will, you sorry sonofabitch." He turned his attention back to the girl. She was in her early twenties, slim, with very dark brown hair pinned up beneath her white cap. "I can guess what he was trying to do," he told her gently. "What I want to know now is whether or not you want me to take the matter to Mr Col — "

The girl's hazel eyes went wide and her mouth dropped open. *"No!"*

Luke spun as Nodeen came at him with a roundhouse right. He ducked under the blow and buried his own right fist in the other man's ample belly. Nodeen made a little grunting sound, another as Luke followed through with a left to the ribs.

Luke came in fast, intending to finish it quickly, but succeeded only in walking straight into a vicious right hook. Pain burst in his head as he lurched backwards, out of reach. Nodeen might be past his prime, he told himself ruefully, but he could still pack a punch.

Luke shook his head in an effort to regain his senses, but Nodeen wasn't about to give him a chance to recover. The bigger man struck him with a left hook to the body and Luke slammed against the wall, only dimly aware of the girl calling for them both to stop in a high, panic-laced screech.

Nodeen came at him again, wearing a thin, sadistic smile, jabbing with his scarred left fist and following through with a powerful right cross. Luke managed to slip the jab and absorb some of the impact of the right with his shoulder. Coming in under the jab, he pounded the giant's ribs and belly, but with little result. While the girl watched through horrified eyes, the bigger man lashed out with a vicious over-hand right that bloodied Luke's mouth and added to the confusion now hampering his thoughts. He pushed Luke away from him, once again slamming him against the wall.

Luke felt the rich silk wallpaper cool against one battered cheek. Over the sound of blood pounding in his ears he heard the girl begging them to stop this before one of them killed the other. He half-fell to one side just in time to avoid the punch that Nodeen had been aiming at his kidneys.

Nodeen's hard right fist hit the wall instead and he muttered something that was part-yelp, part-curse. Luke wheeled around to face him again, launched a right which Nodeen blocked, a left that he didn't, another right that drove the big bastard back on spongy legs.

Luke struck him again and again, aching fists connecting more often than they missed. He didn't care where they were or that this ruckus would likely cost them both their jobs, he just wanted to put the bigger man in his place once and for all, teach him a lesson and teach it *good*.

He lashed out again and again, driving Nodeen back further, further, further . . .

And then, somehow, they both heard the flurry of gunshots that suddenly exploded from someplace upstairs, and even before the echoes had died away, their fight was momentarily forgotten and both of them were racing off to find out what in hell was going on.

4

HELLER and Nodeen burst from the narrow hallway into the spacious lobby. A small crowd of people had gathered at the foot of the stairway, listening as a woman's scream filtered down from one of the upstairs rooms. The security men pushed roughly through the knot of guests before taking the stairs two at a time.

Jess Monroe was standing on the first floor landing. Spotting him, Luke pulled up sharp with Nodeen panting and puffing some distance behind him.

"What is it, Jess?"

The young bellhop looked nervous. "Sounded like shots, Mr Heller. Shots and a scream c-coming from down there!"

"All right, son. Get along downstairs now, and stop anyone else from coming up here until I say so. Got that?"

"Yessir!"

Luke palmed his Colt and waited for Nodeen to reach him. The fight had left them both hot and sweaty, with aching muscles, tender fists and a fair amount of facial and body bruises. As Nodeen wheezed up beside him, Luke began to taste blood in his mouth.

Wordlessly they began to ease along the opulent hallway, each man keeping his back to the wall. The hotel was almost totally silent now, and the silence stretched their taut nerves still tighter. Nodeen hit a loose floorboard and the creak stopped them both in their tracks. Then they caught a sound coming from an open door at the end of the corridor, a moan or wail.

They made it to the door without further event, and after the slightest of pauses, Luke went inside quickly, with his gun cocked. The room was twice the size of his own, and far more richly furnished. Royal blue velvet drapes hung at the floor-to-ceiling windows, which stood open to let in the cool evening air. Rich Oriental rugs covered the hardwood floor, and paintings of the Rocky Mountains decorated oak-panelled walls. A door in the southeast wall led through to a bathroom.

What caught Luke's attention at once, however, was the beautiful Juliet Cameron, who stood in the centre of the room, her body wracked by sobs; the woman, and the bloody, still form of her husband, Austin, who lay sprawled at her feet with his eyes staring vacantly up at the ceiling.

Luke slipped the Colt away and crossed the floor to kneel beside the old man. At first he'd imagined that Austin Cameron had expired through natural causes. As he'd remarked to Mrs Cameron that very afternoon, the old man had certainly appeared in ill health.

Then he realised that Cameron had been shot.

Quickly he checked for a pulse, not that he really expected to find one. A brief examination confirmed that the old man was dead. But why? Was it an accident, or something more; suicide, perhaps, or murder?

Regaining his feet, he went over and pulled the bedspread from the ornate frame and covered the corpse. Then he faced Juliet Cameron, who quickly closed the distance between them and buried her head in his shoulder, her body continuing to tremble and shudder with grief.

Luke held her awkwardly, mind racing, as Nodeen glared at him from the open doorway. "Just what the hell's been goin' on here?" the ex-prizefighter growled.

Luke answered him over one shoulder, voice low and urgent. "Watch your mouth, will you? You can see what's been going on. Just go find Mr Colfax and tell him . . . what we've found. Fetch my girl while you're about it. This woman needs a little company of her own gender."

"But — "

"Just *do* it, Nodeen! *Now!*"

The big man muttered something under his breath, but turned to do as Luke had ordered. As Mrs Cameron continued to weep, he reached up to comfort her, movements awkward and uneasy, and gently urged her across to the bed, where he told her to sit while he fetched her a glass of water.

When he came back out of the bathroom, Mai was standing in the doorway with one tiny hand fisted to her mouth and her large almond eyes locked on the blanket-covered corpse. There hadn't been enough time for Nodeen to have tracked her down and told her to come up; chances were that she'd already been on her way, to be near her man.

He offered her a brief, tight smile and said, "Look after Mrs Cameron for me, will you? I want to take a look around."

Mai tore her gaze away from the body and compassion replaced the horror in her eyes. As she went over and sat beside the woman, reaching out to pat her hand and talk comfortingly to her, Juliet Cameron began to cry again. Luke watched the two women for a moment, then went about his business.

The room had been ransacked. Drawers had been pulled out, the wardrobe stood open, clothes and personal items were strewn everywhere in a careless jumble. Returning to the body, Luke lifted the bedspread and examined Austin Cameron again. The man had been shot twice in the chest at short range, possibly with a small-calibre pistol. He heard voices in the hallway, replaced the spread and stood up.

" . . . yessir, Mr Colfax. I left Heller here an' came right after you . . . "

Luke shook his head. Sounded like Nodeen was struggling to make himself look efficient as he brought the hotel-owner to the murder scene.

The Englishman pulled up short when he reached the doorway. His normally ruddy face was pale and his blue eyes looked haunted. When he saw Cameron's blood beginning to seep through the expensive covering that Luke had used to shroud him, he appeared distinctly nauseous.

"Good God . . . what . . . what on earth has happened here?"

Luke hustled over and took his employer aside. "Lessen I'm mistaken, it looks as if we've got a murder on our hands, Mr Colfax. As soon as Mrs Cameron here calms down a little, I suggest we try to find out exactly what happened."

Colfax couldn't take his eyes from the body and the blood. "My God . . . " he muttered. "You . . . you're sure he's . . . dead?"

"As sure as guns're iron."

"We . . . we'll have to sort this out quickly."

"Of course."

"And discreetly."

"Luke."

Mai's soft voice carried to them

across the room. "Mrs Cameron . . . she would like to talk with you now."

The beautiful young widow appeared to have composed herself. She sat up straight, with a determined look in her eyes. As Luke approached her, he noted the calm assurance which had settled over her. She hadn't exactly shown much regard for her husband earlier on, and after her initial and understandable reaction, she seemed to have accepted his death in much the same manner.

When she sighed, Luke could not help but glance down at the attractive swell of her breasts. It was a hell of a note, but he was a man, after all, and as he had concluded earlier, Juliet Cameron was all woman.

"What happened here, lady?" It was Nodeen.

The beautiful woman brought order to her thoughts. "My . . . husband and I were just returning from dinner. He was tired after . . . this afternoon. You'll recall finding him wandering the grounds earlier this afternoon, Mr Heller?"

Luke nodded.

"Well, w-we had dinner, a few drinks, and decided to turn in for the night. When we got back to the room . . . "

Mai gently took the widow's hand as Luke urged her to continue, Colfax and Nodeen standing tensely behind him, both of them hanging on the woman's every word.

"As we entered the room and Austin began to t-turn up one of the lamps, we . . . we discovered a man going through our possessions. Austin called out, tried to stop him, but, oh, the poor dear was so frail. The man p-pulled a gun from his pocket and sh-shot him . . . " She seemed to be on the verge of breaking down again, and though her body shook for a moment, Juliet Cameron regained her composure. "I screamed and the man ran over to that w-window," she said. "That was the last I saw of him."

"You mean he jus' threw himself off

the balcony?" Nodeen cut in, clearly puzzled.

She shrugged. "Oh, I don't know . . . "

Luke glanced over at the open window to the left of the dresser. He'd check it out in a minute. Meanwhile; "Could you describe the man for us?"

She shrugged again. "I'm not s-sure. The room was still relatively dark, you see . . . " She thought about it for a moment, finally dredging up some details. "He was wearing a big hat pulled low," she decided. "And a bandanna covered most of his lower face."

"That's all?"

"He was a big man, I think . . . about six feet in height and two hundred or so pounds in weight."

Luke went over to the window through which the killer had disappeared and stepped out onto the cool stone balcony beyond. A gentle, refreshing breeze blew some of the death-scent out of his nostrils. Above him the night sky was wide, clear and starry. Directly ahead, maybe half a mile away, timber-studded slopes rose up in a blanket of shadow.

He examined the balcony in the meagre light, found nothing the killer might have left behind him. A thick smudge of ivy crawled up the white stone wall to the left of the balcony, black, not green, in the darkness. Luke reached over, grabbed a handful and tugged at it. He didn't think it was strong enough to support a big man's weight. He thrust his hand deeper into the vine. The rustling of leaves was the only sound. After a moment his probing fingers touched something cold, metallic and slightly curved . . .

He identified a drainage pipe hidden beneath the foliage. *That* would have supported the killer, he thought. Oh, it would still have been a dangerous descent, hard enough in daylight, positively deadly at night. But if a man was desperate enough . . . He peered over the balcony rail. About thirty or forty feet below he made out a flower bed. He stood there for a moment longer. He felt that the man he was after must be an employee. Who else would have known that a drainage pipe ran directly down past this room? The size of the man also seemed to indicate a labourer of some sort, one of the Englishman's guides or hunters, perhaps.

He turned and went back into the room. Colfax had taken over Mai's position beside Mrs Cameron and was speaking to her in a quiet, reassuring tone. Over by the door, Mai was watching anxiously for him to return, and Nodeen was watching her.

"Well?" asked the one-time pugilist.

Luke said, "Let's step outside." When they were back in the hallway he replied. "Anyone on the staff fit the description of this killer?"

Nodeen laughed grimly. "Hell, a dozen of 'em, maybe. Why? You think — ?"

"I'm not sure *what* I think yet. But

you'd better get someone to ride out and fetch the Grey Springs sheriff."

"Mr Colfax ain't gonna like that."

"He doesn't have to."

Nodeen smirked, figuring to give him enough rope to hang himself. "Anythin' else?"

"Yeah. Someone's gonna have to clean up that room and move the dead man over to the icehouse or someplace. Then we'd better set about checking on every man in the place who fits the description Mrs Cameron gave us."

"Aw . . ."

"That's if the sonofabitch hasn't already skinned out. Better check in at the stables to make sure no-one's saddled up and lit out in a hurry tonight."

Nodeen nodded, but before he turned away he dropped one hand on Luke's shoulder and squeezed tightly. "All right, I'll get straight on it. But remember, Mr Detective, we still got some unfinished business . . ."

"Later, Nodeen, later." Luke shrugged

away from him and turned towards Mai, who waited until Nodeen was trudging back along the corridor before saying, "You have been fighting."

"Oh, it was nothing. Leastways nothing compared to *this* business." He ran a hand through his short black hair. "Come on, let's get you back to your room. I've got some investigating to do."

Afterwards, Luke hustled downstairs and out into the night. He wanted to take a look at the flower bed directly beneath the drainage pipe, see if he couldn't scare up some tracks and follow them back to their source. As soon as he reached the spot, however, he realised that he should've moved faster; a group of people had already gathered there to peer up at the murder-room, and were in the process of trampling away whatever tracks there might have been.

" . . . yes, yes, the shots came from up there," a pudgy little man with heavily-oiled hair was saying.

"Yes, gunshots and a series of *the* most blood-curdling screams," an elderly lady in a green evening gown exclaimed to the gathering. "I tell you, it is murder most foul!"

"Murder, my dear Mrs Bavinstock? Only *murder*?" A tall, grey-haired man now held the group's attention. "Why, I understand that it was a gang of robbers who shot their way down the second-floor hallway. One of the staff tells me they killed three people before leaping out of that very window."

Luke bit back a curse. "All right, all right, I think that's enough speculation, don't you? Why don't you folks go on back inside now? There's nothing to see here . . ."

Slowly the crowd began to disperse, still buzzing with excitement as they ambled back to the hotel for more games, drink and gossip about the evening's events. Watching them go, he wondered why Colfax had been so intent on keeping Cameron's murder quiet. It would likely *increase* his business, not ruin it. These society folks had come here for a taste of the wild west. Well, hell, that's exactly what they were getting, and damned if they weren't enjoying it.

The night had turned quite chilly now. It was beginning to sharpen his thinking. Returning to the lobby, he strode across to the reception desk and gestured to one of the clerks, a prissy-looking, middle-aged fellow in a smart, pale grey suit.

"May I help you, Mr Heller?"

"Uh-huh; I want to take a look at the register."

"Why, of course. Is this to do with the murder? Do you have a lead?"

Luke ignored him, concentrating instead on the book the other man placed before him. He began to scan the most recent entries, looking for a familiar name. Barney Phipps had come into his mind out there in the darkness, and he wondered if the little rodent had registered here under one of his old aliases. He was also wondering if the safe-cracker might somehow be involved in the death of Austin Cameron. One thing was certain; it was past time for a long talk with his old, weasel-faced nemesis.

Finding nothing even vaguely familiar about the names in the book, Luke thanked the clerk and turned around just in time to see the very man he was after step into the lobby from the restaurant. No sooner did the two men spot each other, however, than Phipps set off for the bar-room at a run.

"*Hold it!*" Luke yelled.

But the little man was already darting through the doorway and into the crowded bar as Luke began to give chase.

The man from Tombstone fairly burst into the bar-room behind him, just in time to see the weasel-like form shoving through the tangle of wealthy patrons like a man trying to swim against the tide. That he was heading for the casino, and the french windows which led out onto the veranda and possible escape was almost certain.

"*Damn!*"

Doggedly Luke also started shouldering through the crowd, certain now that it was Phipps he was after, and not the fictitious engineer the man had first claimed to be. A friendly drunk grabbed him by one arm — "Buy you a drink, buddy? The name's John Wolfe from Reno, Nevada," — but Luke shook him off and kept moving rapidly through the smoke-filled room.

By the time he reached the casino, Barney Phipps was legging it to one of the open windows forty feet ahead, just like he'd figured. Luke dodged a couple of roulette players and followed him out into the darkness, determined not to let the little rat give him the slip.

Cool night air dried the sweat on his face as he came to a halt amidst all the now-vacant tables and chairs. He looked left, saw nothing, looked right —

Barney was weaving quickly around all the tables clustered down there, hitting a few and sending chair-legs skidding across night-moist flagstones. Once more Luke called for him to hold it; once more the weasel ignored him and just kept going.

Gritting his teeth, the Tombstone detective went after him, long legs pumping, lungs working at a feverish rate.

Phipps deliberately overturned a chair in his path. Luke leapt over it and kept going. The weasel was down off the veranda now, slipping a little on the rolling, dew-slick grass. Stubbornly Luke kept after him, pulses racing like war-drums, furiously sucking in clear, thin high-country air as he slowly but inexorably closed the distance between them.

The light out here was poor now, star- and moon-glow only, nothing of the Mountain View's strong, artificial yellow light. If Luke didn't catch his man soon, Phipps might yet escape, either into the darkness or beyond the cultivated maze of bushes and shrubs now growing ever-closer.

Phipps topped a gentle rise, went racing helter-skelter down the other side, hit a neat gravel path in a spray of stones and followed it around a curve screened by brush. Luke slipped once, righted himself, followed with his boots crunching gravel in a string of quick, long strides. As he came around the curve, however, he knew instinctively that something was about to go badly wrong.

The bushes off to his left gave a shiver. He heard the leaves rustling together quite clearly. He tried to pull up, realising that he'd been suckered, turned just as a big man — too big to be Barney Phipps — came out of the brush with a lead-lined sap in one gloved fist and struck him right across the forehead.

"Uh . . . "

Luke went backwards. The sap had opened a cut on his forehead; he could feel blood warm against his skin. The man came in again, too fast for him to pick out any details or do anything about it, and the sap struck once more.

Luke went down just as the gravel path came up to meet him. He was unconscious by the time the two of them connected.

★ ★ ★

For a long time there was nothing but the empty darkness. Then the dream began to fill his head like so much coloured smoke, and he was back in Missouri on January 25th 1875, trying desperately to call off the attack on 'Castle James' before Frank Johnson's potflare blew up; and, as usual, failing.

It was as the 'Grecian fire' exploded inside the Samuels' place that Luke gave a little start and came suddenly and completely awake. "Oooh . . . "

Coloured sparks danced across his eyelids. His head was pounding in time to a funeral dirge. But he knew without having to open his eyes and look around that someone had found him out there where the man with the lead-lined sap had left him — possibly for dead — and brought him back to the hotel. There was a feather mattress beneath him now, not the hard, unyielding earth, and a cool, damp cloth draped across his tender forehead.

For a full minute he lay perfectly still, trying to collect his thoughts. But all he had were questions. Exactly how did Barney Phipps fit into this business, if at all? The man with the sap . . . Was he one of the little man's accomplices, or maybe Austin Cameron's killer? Thinking of Cameron made him open his eyes and try to get up. He had no way of knowing how long he'd been out, but there was work to do, guests and staff alike to question —

"Be still, Luke. It is not good that you should try moving around so soon."

With a groan he lay back and turned his head against the cool pillow, allowing the cloth on his forehead to slip aside. He was in his room, and Mai was sitting at his side, concern in the frown she wore on her otherwise smooth face. "I'll . . . be all right in a minute. Anyway, there's work to be done."

"It *has* been done," she told him firmly. "The sheriff from Grey Springs arrived. The murder is his responsibility now." She leaned forward to look into his bloodshot green eyes, inspecting him for any lingering injuries. "Just rest, Luke. And tell me what happened."

He did, and when he was finished she gave a nod. "The desk clerk, he said that you were searching for this man, this Phipps, and that you chased him into the bar. When you didn't return within half an hour, Mr Colfax sent out some men to find you." Suddenly her face crumpled a little and her bottom lip worked hard for a while. "Oh, Luke . . . I thought they had killed *you*, too!"

He winced ruefully. "Not hardly. Oh, they had a damn' good try, whoever they are. But . . . " He paused, noticing pale grey light at the window. "Just how long was I out, anyway?"

She shrugged. "Some time."

"Couple hours?"

"Six."

That settled it. Regardless of Mai's protestations, he'd rested long enough. He sat up slowly, fighting the wave of nausea that swept over him, sucked in a couple of deep breaths, then thrust up from the bed.

Standing up without wanting to fall right down again required a sight more effort. When he thought he had it licked, he went over to the washstand and splashed his face a few times.

"You should be seen by a doctor," Mai admonished. "I did the best for you that I could, but . . . "

"Your best is good enough," he said.

Anyway, he knew from experience that he'd feel better after a shave and some food. While Mai watched with obvious disapproval, he lathered his face and began the morning ritual, admittedly a mite slower than usual.

Drying his face and upper body ten minutes later, he slipped into a fresh shirt, quickly knotted a tie and buttoned his vest. His shoulder harness and holster came next, and when that was buckled, the Oriental girl helped him shrug into his jacket.

Together they went to grab some breakfast.

5

JIM NODEEN was loitering in the lobby, idly picking his teeth with a matchstick. When he saw Luke and Mai coming down the staircase arm in arm he swaggered over to meet them.

"Well, well, well; if it isn't the big-city detective. Have a good night's sleep, Heller?"

Luke grimaced. "Thanks to a feller with a sap, I don't remember much about it."

"Well, that's what you get if you go off chasin' shadows, I guess." Nodeen flicked the matchstick into a nearby plantpot. He looked hollow-eyed this morning, and even more haggard than usual. "But I gotta tell you somethin', boy; I jus' don't know what we'd have done without your help las' night. All them questions that had to be ast, all the legwork . . ."

Ignoring the sarcasm, Luke answered, "Did you turn anything up, though?"

"About the Cameron business? Not a thing. Oh, we got plenty fellers who fit the killer's description, but half of 'em got alibis and the other half got no motive."

"I thought the motive was robbery."

"That's what I'm sayin'. These rich people here; why should they go stealin' pennies from anyone else?"

"For the thrill of it, maybe?"

"Nah, you're chasin' shadows again."

"Well, what about the staff?"

Nodeen's broad shoulders rose and fell in a shrug. "They got no quarrel with the wages Colfax pays 'em. He might be a queer old bird at times, but he treats his staff square enough. Why risk losin' a good job an' salary, an' gettin' caught, jus' to knock over one stupid room?"

It was Luke's turn to use sarcasm. "You think the old man shot himself, then? After he and his wife ransacked their room?"

"*You're* the detective, not me. Anyway, Ward's handlin' it now."

"Ward?"

"Deb Ward. The sheriff."

Luke felt Mai's grip on his arm tighten, and knew she wanted to get away from the other man. "All right, Nodeen. It's out of our hands. But that doesn't mean we can't give this lawdog some help."

The former pugilist seemed unimpressed by the suggestion. "I've had my crack at helpin' him out," he growled. "I was up all night, askin' questions, remember? Anyway, the old man wants to see you."

"Colfax?"

"Uh-huh. Like *now*."

As Nodeen lumbered off, Luke and Mai exchanged a glance. Breakfast, it seemed, would have to wait. Together they went along the hallway towards the Englishman's office, and when they reached the door, Luke tapped a brief tattoo.

"Enter."

Luke opened the door and they went inside. A lemon-faced woman of middle years was over by a file cabinet with a sheaf of papers in her hand. She was tall, a little heavy around the hips, with greying hair gathered into a bun. She eyed Luke and Mai over the small, wire-framed glasses she had pinched onto her nose. Although Luke had never seen the woman before, it was a pretty safe bet that she was the Englishman's secretary.

"Ah, it's Mr Heller, isn't it?" she said with a brisk nod. "Mr Colfax has been expecting you." She gestured to his forehead, and the angry-looking bump and cut visible there. "Will you be needing the services of a physician for that, do you think?"

He shook his head. "I think I'll pull through."

"Very well. I'll announce you. Your, ah, lady-friend may wait for you here."

She went over to a half-glass door in the left-side wall, knocked and went on through. Luke heard a low-voiced exchange, then she came back and said, "Go right in."

He did as he was told. As he'd expected, Colfax' office reflected his obvious love of luxury. The carpet was thick, the pictures on the wood-panelled walls were original oils, not prints, and there was a well-stocked drinks cabinet beside the door. Clean, fresh morning sunlight spilled in through a large, barred window, and just to the left of the Englishman's wide, paper-cluttered desk sat a big, heavy grey Jenks & Millbush safe.

Colfax, seated at the desk, watched him come in and close the door behind him. He didn't look quite so nauseous this morning, but he was still pale and worried. A cigar was balanced on the lip of an ashtray to his right, sending a string of fragrant grey smoke up to the ceiling. "Mr Heller. My goodness, you had us worried last night. What on earth happened to you? Did you ... did you tangle with Mr Cameron's killer?" He spoke the last word softly, not wishing it to carry beyond the table.

Luke shook his head. "I'm not really sure *what* happened yet," he responded honestly. Briefly he recounted the events which led to his being knocked out.

"Then you are sure that the man you chased really is this, ah, Phipps?"

"Uh-huh. Why else would he have run when I tried to brace him if he didn't have something to hide?"

Colfax reached for his cigar and took a deep drag. When he looked up again he said, "Please, Mr Heller, take a seat. I think we have to talk. Urgently. This business last night . . . it could be disastrous unless we deal with it quickly and efficiently. Five guests have already checked out this morning alone, and others are threatening to do the same."

As Luke took the weight off he said, "I understand the sheriff came out to handle things."

"Yes, and he'll be coming back

later today, but . . . " Colfax gestured impatiently. "You have a saying out here, Mr Heller, a bit earthy, I'll grant you, but accurate enough in the circumstances. Sheriff Ward couldn't find his backside with both hands, sir. I doubt if he could even catch a cold! This Cameron business is entirely out of his league."

"Then what are you suggesting?"

Colfax took another drag on the cigar and leaned forward across the desk. "I'll be candid with you, sir; we need to be seen to be looking for this killer, if only to allay the fears of the other guests and uphold the reputation of the hotel. That is why I am prepared to offer you a, uh, 'bounty' of five hundred dollars over and above your agreed salary if you clear this matter up within the week."

Luke considered the Englishman's offer poker-faced. Finally he said, "That's a pretty tall order, Mr Colfax."

"Of course it is. But surely so was tracing young Nancy Lawrence from

Arizona to San Francisco?" The dapper little man set his cigar aside. "Look, let us understand each other, Mr Heller . . . Luke . . . If we cannot apprehend this killer — and for all we know he could be miles from here by now — then the very least we can do is *appear* to be trying to find him. The guests want reassurance. That is what I want you to give them."

Luke ran everything through his mind again. There wasn't an awful lot to go on; if he pulled it off, he'd have earned every penny of his so-called bounty. But what the hell; he'd been prepared to lend the Grey Springs sheriff a hand for free — why shouldn't he get paid while he was at it?

"All right, Mr Colfax, I'll give it a go, but obviously I can't give you any guarantees . . ."

"Just do your best, Mr . . . Luke. For the benefit of the guests, be seen to be doing your best."

"Fair enough."

"And, uh ... about this *other* matter ... "

Luke raised one eyebrow. "Phipps? Let's just hope I've made him think twice before he tries anything nefarious around here, shall we?"

With a nod he got to his feet and left the office. Outside he collected Mai, and as they headed for the staff dining room, he quickly told the young Oriental girl the gist of his conversation with the Englishman.

When he was through, Mai peered up at him with a frown. "Do you think you can find this killer, Luke? Nodeen says — "

"Forget what Nodeen says. If the killer's still in these parts to be found," he replied, "I'll find him."

She tightened her grip on his arm. "Just be careful. That is all I ask."

He looked down at her. "I will," he assured her gently. "And Mai, while we're about it ... thanks for patching me up last night. I'm real sorry this trip hasn't exactly gone according to plan yet, but it will, just as soon as I get this job out of the way. I promise."

He was right; a good breakfast concluded the recovery his wash and shave had started, and by the time he pushed his empty plate aside and sat back from the trestle table in the staff dining room, the pounding in his head was almost gone and he'd regained his full sense of balance. He was still feeling a little fragile, but better than he had been at sunrise.

As they left the dining room and prepared to split up, Mai asked if there was anything she could do to help him. After a moment's thought he nodded. "Yeah; keep your eye out for Barney Phipps." Quickly he described the man, adding that she should enlist Jess Monroe's help, too. "If either of you find him, just come fetch me straight away. Got that? Don't do anything to make him suspicious, just come and fetch me."

She nodded. "I understand." Then she was gone.

Luke scanned the lobby. The desk looked pretty quiet, so he concluded that the initial rush of guests checking out had slowed down. A quick look through the double doors at the grounds fronting the hotel told him that the day was going to be a beauty, a day of picnics and laughter, not an investigation of murder.

But somebody had to do it, so he went over to the desk clerk and asked if the management had moved Austin Cameron's widow to a different room. They had; she was in 217 now. Luke thanked the clerk and went upstairs to find it. With nowhere better to start, he might just as well see if the beautiful Juliet Cameron had remembered anything else about her husband's murder that might offer him some direction.

When he reached his destination, he paused before knocking. This was going to take some tact; talking to the recently-bereaved nearly always did. He rapped his knuckles discreetly against the door panel and a moment later the door swung open.

"Yes?"

For just a moment, Luke was thrown off-balance. He'd been expecting to see Juliet Cameron, not a man. He wondered if he had the right room. Before he could respond, however, Juliet Cameron herself appeared behind the man, her pale face inquisitive.

"Who is it, Anthony?"

Luke cut in before the other man had a chance. "It's me, Mrs Cameron, Luke Heller. I don't mean to intrude, but I was hoping to ask you a few questions about last night. I can come back later if you're, ah, busy."

Juliet came forward in a swish of silk. She was dressed in black, as befitted a recent widow, but the outfit clung to the smooth, fluid contours of her slim waist and flared hips, and the sombre colour only made the corn-yellow of her hair and the sky-blue of her eyes more apparent.

"Please, Mr Heller. If I can be of

any further help . . . "

"Perhaps I should leave you alone," said the man she'd called Anthony.

Luke glanced at him, wondering who in hell he was. Seeing the speculation in his eyes, Juliet at last thought to make introductions. "Of course not, Anthony. Stay. Please. Mr Heller, this is Anthony Brandon. Anthony is — *was* — my husband's attorney back in New York. His practice handles much of the business for the bank of which my husband was president."

Brandon offered his hand and as they shook, Luke sized him up. The lawyer was tall and handsome, about thirty years of age. He had dark, curly hair and a square jaw. Wearing an expensive three-piece suit of iron-grey cloth, he appeared to be well-proportioned, striking and prosperous. There was something about him that Luke found hard to trust, however, but maybe he was just smelling a rat somewhere.

"Kind of a ways off your usual stamping-grounds, aren't you, Mr

Brandon?" he remarked.

"I just checked in last night," the lawyer replied as Luke stepped inside and Brandon closed the door behind him. "I had no idea that Austin and Juliet were here until I heard the terrible news just a few minutes ago. Naturally, I came right up to offer my condolences and see if I could be of any assistance."

"Of course."

Luke glanced around. The room was similar to the one in which Cameron had died the previous night, except that it was filled with the scent of freshly-cut flowers, which Colfax had probably sent up as a token of his sympathy.

"Now, Mr Heller," Juliet said, moving across to a sofa by the window. "How may I help you? I went through all of this with the sheriff last night, for all the good I fear it will do."

Luke turned his attention to the woman, thinking that this whole business was just a little too convenient for comfort. He still wasn't sure what to make of it, though, and he knew better than to jump to conclusions. "I know that, ma'am. But sometimes you remember more *after* the event. I know it's not easy, but if you think back now, do you recall anything at all that might prove useful, something you might have overlooked at the time . . . ?"

She produced a small lace handkerchief from her reticule and dabbed at her nose. "As I told you last night, my husband and I were returning from dinner. He was tired and we had decided to make it an early evening. As we came through the door and Austin turned up one of the lamps, we saw a man going through our dresser drawers. When Austin called out and tried to stop him . . . " With a shudder she bowed her head.

Luke waited a moment before going on. "Would you describe the man for me again, please?"

She did, not really adding much beyond what she'd said the night before; that he was tall and heavy, and that his features were hidden beneath a bandanna and a hat, pulled low.

"Did you catch the colour of his hair at all?"

She thought for a couple of seconds. "N-not that I remember."

He tried a different tack. "Do you know whether or not the killer got away with anything?"

"Nothing."

"You're sure? No jewellery or cash? Important papers, maybe?"

"I . . . I have accounted for everything."

He kept his sigh soft, but it was frustrating as hell to keep coming up against brick walls all the time. Still, maybe he was making headway and just didn't know it. He thanked the woman and promised to do everything he could to bring her husband's killer to justice, then turned and headed for the door.

Brandon's voice stopped him. "Mr Heller. If there's anything I can do to help . . . "

Luke looked across at him. Tall and heavy, he thought. And he'd only arrived last night. "Thanks," he replied as he let himself out. "I appreciate the offer, Mr Brandon. But I think you might be of more value here, looking after Mrs Cameron."

The lawyer nodded. "If you're sure . . ."

"I am."

Out in the hallway he cautioned himself against making any premature judgements. Maybe Brandon's turning up just in time to comfort the grieving widow *was* coincidence. But Luke knew from experience that few things were ever as clear-cut as they seemed.

He went back down to the lobby and helped himself to the register. It wasn't hard to find Brandon's name; it was the most recent entry in the book. He ran his eyes across the page, located the man's room number and then called the desk clerk over. Prissy was on duty again. As the middle-aged clerk came across, Luke smelled his cheap cologne and hair oil and had to fight against wrinkling his nose.

"Can I help you, Mr Heller?"

"I'd like the pass key."

Prissy frowned. "Oh. Well, I'm not sure. I mean, normally I would require specific instructions from Mr Colfax himself before handing that over."

"I haven't got time for that."

"You have a valid reason for needing it, I assume?"

Luke's patience ran dry. "Look, just hand it over — and keep this to yourself."

The clerk stayed where he was for a moment. Finally he turned and went away. When he came back he handed the pass key over without a word.

"Thanks."

The man from Tombstone was just pushing away from the desk when he caught sight of Jess Monroe. Motioning the young man over, he slipped the key into his pocket and crossed the lobby to meet him halfway.

"'Morning, Jess."

"Mr Heller. Help you?"

"I was just wondering if you could shed any light on what happened last night."

The kid's eyes went big. "About the murder, you mean?"

"About the feller who gave me this lump on the head."

"I thought it was all one an' the same thing."

Heller sighed. "Maybe it is, Jess. I just don't know yet. Well?"

The boy thought. "Can't really help you much. It was a wild kind of night, after all. The desk clerk saw you chase that other feller into the bar an' called Mr Nodeen. When you didn't come back, couple of us went out lookin' for you. That's it."

"Did my girl find you?"

"Yessir. She told me to keep an eye out for a little feller with a face like a rat. Philips, wasn't it?"

"Phipps."

"Uh, yeah."

"Thanks, son."

"Anytime, Mr Heller."

Luke watched him move away, then started back up the stairs to the second floor, where Brandon's room was located.

He had no compunction about going through the other man's belongings. He was out to find a killer, after all. But he had no desire to get caught whilst he was at it; that's why he'd suggested that Brandon stay with Juliet, to keep him out of the way. Even so, he intended to be as quick and as thorough as he could, then get the hell out of there. If Brandon was implicated in this business somehow, Luke certainly did not want to tip his hand until he was ready. If the man was innocent — and there was still every possibility that he was — then there was no need for him to know he had ever been under suspicion.

Brandon's room was the first one he came to. He knocked at the door, just in case the attorney had returned to the room after all. There was no response.

He checked the hallway. It was deserted. He listened at the door. There was no sound. Quickly he produced the pass key and let himself inside.

The room was large, set out along much the same lines as the Cameron quarters. He closed the door behind him as softly as he could and relocked it. Then he ghosted across to the ornate, heavy chest of drawers and began a systematic search.

The chest yielded nothing.

He checked through the wardrobe. Empty. Maybe Brandon hadn't started unpacking yet.

The lawyer's suitcases weren't hard to find. The luggage was so big and so expensive that it would have been kind of hard to miss. He crossed the bright, quiet room, turned the first case onto its side and worked the catches.

Luke whistled softly. Brandon had sure come prepared. He'd never seen so many clothes. He rummaged through the case but came up empty. Not that he was completely sure exactly what he was hoping to find.

He re-secured the case and opened its companion. More clothes. The lawyer was a veritable fashion-plate.

Luke searched as completely as he could. Suddenly his questing fingers met the cool hardness of curved metal. He knew exactly what he'd found even before he withdrew it from the neatly-folded shirts and underwear beneath which it had been buried.

It was a five-shot, single-action New Line Police Colt in .38 calibre, kind of strange baggage for a New York attorney to be carrying.

He checked the weapon. It wasn't loaded. He sniffed at the barrel, trying to detect whether or not it had been fired recently. There was no smell of burnt powder on it, but that came as no surprise; the weapon had been cleaned thoroughly — and not so very long ago, either.

He replaced the weapon, rearranged the case, relocked it and put it back where he'd found it. But where did that leave *him*? All right, so he'd found a gun. But what did that mean? Not one damn' thing. He'd need a darn-sight more than that before he could say he'd found his man.

He checked the bathroom. Nothing. But just as he was about to leave, he spotted a book on the bedside cabinet. On impulse he went across to it, picked it up, checked the spine. It was Governor Wallace's novel of the time of Christ, *Ben Hur*.

He opened the book, riffled its pages. Brandon had marked his place with a folded sheet of paper. Heller was about to let it go, then thought better of it and decided to check it. He had no intention of reading another man's correspondence if it appeared innocuous. But then he saw who had sent it.

Juliet Cameron.

Something unpleasant began to uncoil in Heller's guts. He checked the date of the letter. It had been written about two months earlier. Hurriedly he ran his green eyes over its contents.

' . . . so good to see you again, dearest Anthony. Though I should not confess it, life with Austin can be so dull. It is only the memory of the good times we shared that keeps me sane. We experienced so much together that I hope you cannot forget what we meant to each other any more than I . . . '

Luke digested that. What did it mean? That Brandon and Juliet were more than just good friends was now obvious. But did that automatically implicate them in Austin Cameron's murder? Of course not. But it gave the Tombstone detective an awful lot to think about.

Until he heard footsteps coming along the hallway outside, that was.

Brandon? It was possible. He slipped the folded sheet of paper back into the book and went across to the door.

He held his breath until the footsteps went past.

It was time to get out of there. Things were starting to add up, but he didn't have a total yet.

He unlocked the door and let himself back into the hallway. He had just relocked the door behind him when Jim Nodeen came lumbering up the stairs. As soon as the former pugilist spotted him standing there, his piggy little eyes narrowed down still further.

"Well, looky here," Nodeen said slowly, his low voice like gravel skittering across gravel. "Jus' what do you think *you're* doin'?"

Luke met his gaze without looking away. He didn't think the other man had seen him come out of Brandon's room, and if possible he intended to keep as much of this investigation as he could private.

"Just taking a look around," he said after a moment.

Nodeen's mouth cracked into the kind of smile you normally spell

S-N-A-R-L. "Jus' takin' a look around, huh?" he repeated. "You mean to say you ain't got it all solved yet, Mr Detective?"

Luke thought back to the search he'd just made and cracked a humourless smile of his own. "Well, you *could* say I'm still on the case," he said. Then he pushed past the other man and went on downstairs, trying to make sense out of what he had so far.

6

LUKE worried at the facts for most of what remained of the day, but knew he needed more than the rather flimsy evidence and half-formed hunches he had so far. Things were dovetailing just a little too neatly, for one thing, and he was sure that Juliet Cameron and Anthony Brandon were too intelligent to have orchestrated such a seemingly obvious crime.

But what if they *weren't*?

Luke had no intention of underestimating *them*, but could it be that they had underestimated the intelligence of the folks who would be investigating the murder out here? It wouldn't be the first time an Easterner had turned out to be too smart for his — or her — own good.

There was something else he'd

noticed during his investigation so far, too, and he found that puzzling. He didn't know what to make of it yet, but he sure intended to find out.

By the middle of the afternoon, the effects of the lead-lined sap began to make themselves felt again, and he went up to his room and stretched out on the bed. Almost before he knew it, he was asleep.

For once his sleep was dreamless. There was no 'Castle James' to disturb his rest, no Grecian fire, no Zerelda James with half of her right arm dangling by a thread, just pure, unbroken darkness and silence.

He awoke refreshed some indeterminate time later, got up, splashed cold water on his face and then checked the time. It was a little after six o'clock in the evening.

He collected Mai from her room and together they went down to the staff dining room to grab some supper. Mai seemed a little less troubled than she had earlier; as they ate she told him that she had made arrangements to spend the evening with a couple of the off-duty maids, who were local girls anxious to hear news of the outside world, and after the meal Luke left her to it while he reported for the evening shift.

He still couldn't stop worrying at the facts he'd uncovered and the theories he'd started forming about Austin Cameron's death, though. Perhaps it really was an attempted burglary that had gone hideously wrong. Perhaps the killer really *had* lit out for pastures new. But somehow Luke doubted it. There was more to this business than met the eye.

He kicked off his shift with a slow stroll through the ground floor that took in the bar and gaming room with an occasional detour through the lobby and dining room as well. He spotted Jim Nodeen in the bar, and guessed that the giant had already started to indulge his excessive appetite for alcohol.

The evening wore on to the sounds of spinning roulette wheels and the cheerful clink of expensive glassware. By nine o'clock the gaming room was packed to capacity and the bar was equally congested. The air grew stuffy and vibrant with chatter. Guttering oil-lamps bathed each opulent room a rich, deep amber. If Austin Cameron's murder had upset any of the other guests, Luke had yet to see any evidence of it.

It was around nine-thirty that the former Pinkerton man spotted a familiar face in the crowd.

Oh, the lean, lanky figure had changed some, sure. He was older, for one thing, about forty-two or -three now. He was wearing a fine dark suit instead of the dirty range-gear in which Luke had last seen him, and his dark hair was now flecked with grey, but there was no mistaking Henry Barrow. Henry was missing the lobe off his right ear, and a light scar still showed beneath the tan of his skin, running from what was left of the ear to the corner of his mouth. His hollow cheeks were clean-shaven and his eyes were set so deep in his head that shadows seemed to fall like miniature curtains across them. Barrow's high forehead was emphasized by his receding hairline. The hair was combed straight back with no apparent parting.

Luke frowned, immediately on the alert. He did not exactly have a photographic memory, but there were some old reprobates you just didn't forget, and Henry Barrow was one of them.

On impulse he shouldered through the crowd and headed for the bar. He found Nodeen sipping beer just inside the doorway and hustled across to him.

"I think we might be in for some trouble," he said quietly.

Nodeen regarded him closely over the lip of his schooner, his manner slow and thoughtful. At last he said, "Well, what the hell do you 'spect *me* to do about it? I'm off-duty."

Luke bit back a curse. "I mean it, Nodeen. This could be serious. Look, you see that feller over yonder in the dark suit? That's Henry Barrow, a road-agent I crossed trails with a few years back."

Nodeen only sneered. "So?"

"So we've already got a known safe-cracker running around here someplace. Now we've got a sonofabitch who's stolen just about everything from hair-oil to gold-dust. You think that's a coincidence?"

Nodeen shrugged, his movements slow and ponderous. He was obviously feeling no pain. "Boy, you got one heck of an imagination, I'll say that for you. But you're gonna have to learn to stop jumpin' at shadows."

"Look, just — "

Luke broke off as Henry Barrow quickly checked his immediate surroundings, then headed for the lobby. Whatever he'd been doing in the casino had no connection with gambling. It was almost as if the sonofabitch had been keeping watch for someone.

Luke turned his attention back to Nodeen. "You'd better go fetch Colfax while I keep an eye on our friend there," he said tightly.

"Aw, go fetch Colfax yourself," Nodeen replied, belching foul breath into his face. "I'm not your messenger-boy."

Luke's jaw-muscles shifted beneath the tan of his skin, but there was no point in arguing about it; he *would* alert the Englishman himself.

He left the heady atmosphere of the bar and gaming room behind him and crossed the lobby in a series of long-legged strides. He made it halfway down the corridor leading to Colfax's quarters before someone came out of the shadows behind him and pressed the barrel of a handgun hard against the small of his back.

"All right, that's far enough."

Luke pulled up sharply and slowly raised his hands to shoulder-height without having to be told.

"I had a feelin' you spotted me jus' now," said the man behind him. "My Christ, Heller, but you're a hard-headed bastard. I thought I'd finished you last night."

Luke sighed tiredly, trying to figure a way out of this new predicament. "I'm real sorry to disappoint you, Henry." He turned his head slowly so that he could see the lanky man over one shoulder. "Mind if I ask you what it is you're doing here?"

Henry Barrow laughed but kept the gun-barrel firm against his spine. "What does it look like? I'm on vacation."

Luke snorted. "Look, let's not kid each other, Henry. I know you just about as well as I know myself. The Pinkertons alone've got a file on you that's an inch thick. They still talk about you and your larcenous habits from Missouri to the Indian Nations." He paused. "Can I take it that five and a half years in Leavenworth didn't exactly show you the error of your ways?"

"Oh, you don't have to worry 'bout me, Heller. I've gone straight, all right. Straight into the big-time. Y'see, I'm gettin' just a little too old for raidin' banks an' stagecoaches like I used to. I figure to pick up my money an easier way from now on."

"And this is it?"

"This is it. But that's enough gab. Start walkin'. Real easy, now, down to Colfax's office."

With no alternative, Luke did as he was told. When they reached the office door, Barrow stretched cautiously around him and knocked. "Open up. It's me; Henry. And I've brought company."

A short, fat man with a bald head opened the door. Luke had never seen him before in his life. He asked Barrow what the hell Luke was doing there and Barrow told him. He then searched Luke quickly and thoroughly, found and relieved him of his .45, then tossed the weapon into the waste basket on the other side of the room.

As he was shoved deeper into the office, the man from Tombstone surveyed the scene in Colfax's room. It was a disaster. The place had been ransacked. Drawers had been wrenched out and their contents emptied onto the expensive Oriental carpet. Much of the furniture had also been overturned.

Barney Phipps rose from where he'd been kneeling beside the Jenks & Millbush safe. The little rodent had obviously been trying to open the heavy iron depository with the skills he'd acquired during his lifetime of crime. So far, however, all his efforts appeared to have been in vain.

Now he looked at Luke wide-eyed and startled. "Judas . . . it's Heller!"

"Relax," said Barrow. "I got him before he got us."

Besides Barrow, the fat man and Barney Phipps, two other men were also in the room, not counting John Colfax, who looked much the worse for wear. The Englishman's face was mottled with bruises. One eye had swollen shut, and blood was leaking from his nose and mouth. He appeared to be insensible.

Luke's teeth clenched in a sudden, fiery rage. It wasn't hard to see what had happened here. These men had tried to beat the combination of the safe out of the hotel owner. Having knocked him unconscious or worse in the process, Barney Phipps was now trying to break the secret of that combination himself.

The two men who still flanked Colfax were of medium height and build, and wore well-used range-clothes. One of them had Indian or Mexican blood, judging from his swarthy complexion and raven-black hair. The other was pale, with white-blond hair. Both were in their late thirties.

"*Damn!*" exclaimed the fellow with the white-blond hair. "How much longer you gonna be, Barney?"

"Who knows? All night, at this rate."

"You mean you can't open it? I thought you said — "

Barney Phipps wheeled irritably on the other man. "They haven't built the safe I can't open yet, Paget!" he said in a low, dangerous voice. "But this is one of the newer models. 'Til I get the hang of some of the modifications they've made, this is gonna take time."

The fellow with the white-blond hair, Paget, threw a glance at Luke. "Well, time's about the one thing we ain't got, Barney."

The weasel-faced safe-cracker stared at him for a long, tense moment. At last he reached a decision. "All right," he said reluctantly. "Casey, fetch me that satchel."

Henry Barrow stepped forward, his expression one of alarm. "Hey, now, Barney, I thought we said we'd only use that there dynamite as a last resort."

"This is the last resort," Phipps replied angrily. "Face it; Colfax won't give us the combination and I could twist that dial all night before I strike lucky."

"But as soon as that dynamite goes off —"

"Yeah, I know; everyone in the place'll know the safe's been blown." He thought some more. "I'll try to keep it quiet as I can, pack the dynamite for localized effect. But we'll still have to move fast. Best fetch our horses around back, Paget. Rio, go with him. Casey; where's that satchel?"

The fat man who had searched Heller quickly crossed the room with a worn carpetbag in one hand. Phipps dug dynamite from the satchel and Casey's eyes got big as he hurriedly backed away from the explosives. So intent was he on watching Phipps' movements, in fact, that he failed to look where he was going, and he suddenly stumbled on one of the over-turned chairs.

With Paget and the dark-haired Rio already heading for the door, Luke figured he'd never get a better chance.

He shoved Barrow roughly to one

side. Taken completely by surprise, Barrow yelped and lost his balance. Barney Phipps shouted *"Get that bastard!"* and Casey came in with his big fists swinging.

He rushed straight into a hammering right cross that made his nose fragment. Even as he started howling, Heller kicked the fat man square between the legs. But Paget and Rio were already closing on him from behind.

As Casey sank to the floor whimpering, Luke whirled to face this new threat and lashed out at Rio with a straight right fist that missed its target by inches. The other man hit him once, then launched a kick that knocked his legs out from under him. Rio tried to follow it up with another kick, this time at Luke's head, but the detective grabbed the boot before it could connect and twisted, bringing a cry of pain as his assailant tumbled backward.

It turned into a real rough-house then.

As Luke leapt to his feet, he

connected with a left-right combination from Paget that sent him staggering again. He recovered almost at once and started giving as good as he'd got. It was a valiant but futile effort, though. He wasn't outclassed, just out-numbered, and before he could do much more damage, Henry Barrow stepped up behind him and brought a small but heavy vase down hard on his head.

As the vase shattered, Heller sank to his knees. Dazed, shaking his head to clear it, he tried to rise back to his feet but just could not make his body obey orders. Above him, the two rowdies closed upon him fast, each grabbing an arm and dragging him to his feet. Barrow and Phipps watched sadistically as Casey, still whining, struggled upright.

"Seems we owe you somethin', Heller," Barrow growled as he slapped Luke a vicious back-hand blow. "And I think we'll let Casey here pay you off while Barney gets ready to blow the safe."

Phipps went to work doing just that as Casey closed the space between himself and the detective. Although the blood from the man's mashed nose had slowed to a trickle, his face was still a mess. He stood in front of Luke and grinned crookedly, his dark eyes alight with cruelty.

Luke forced himself to meet the other man's expression with a grim smile. After all, if he was going to take a beating, he might just as well earn it.

"I wonder," he said after clearing his throat. "Is your mother as ugly as you, Casey?"

Casey went mad then. "*Sonofabitch!*" he roared.

What followed was not pleasant.

Some little while later, they let him fall to his knees, from his knees onto his face. They thought he'd lost consciousness and they were very nearly right. But somehow he had compartmentalised all the pain the little fat man had dished out and was clinging to his reeling senses, knowing that he could do nothing else if he were to stand any chance of catching up with them again in the not-too-distant future.

Still, if they wanted to believe that he was out of it, he was not about to argue. He hurt like hell. There was not one part of him that *didn't* hurt. He needed some recovery time, and this was it.

Phipps finished work on the safe. He had packed dynamite close to the door's lock and hinges. Fuses trailed from it like dead worms.

"You boys'd better go fetch those horses," the safe-cracker said at last. "I'm all through here. Casey, go with 'em. I doubt you got a decent run left in you."

As Paget and Rio left the room with the short fat man trailing behind them with one hand to his nose and the other nursing his tender groin, Phipps said, "Best get yourself outside, Henry. An' remember; we're gonna have to work fast, here. Soon as the safe blows, we empty it an' run, simple as that."

"Right. What about Heller an' Colfax?"

"What about 'em?"

"You want I should drag 'em outside? We leave 'em in here an' the explosion's like to kill 'em, localized or not."

Phipps thought about that. Robbery was one thing. Cold-blooded murder . . . that was something else.

"All right," he replied. "We got some time to kill anyway, I guess. You take Heller, I'll take the Limey."

Down on the floor, Luke tensed himself. He was younger than the two would-be robbers, younger and faster. And because they thought he was unconscious, he had the element of surprise, too. But when Barrow grabbed him under the arms and dragged him across the thick carpet and out into the ante-room, he realised that the beating had left him as weak as a kitten. He could do nothing but lie there and let Henry

Barrow haul him around like a sack of flour.

The owlhoot left him stretched out on the far side of the ante-room. The carpet felt rough against his battered cheek. A moment later he saw Barney Phipps loom above him through the slits of his eyes and dump the unconscious Colfax beside him.

Phipps hurried over to the window and opened it wide. Barrow crossed to the door and looked out into the corridor. Genteel music drifted in from the dining room, where a string quartet played for the benefit of the guests. Barrow took out a turnip watch and checked the time. On the floor, Luke tried manfully to shrug off his aches and pains and roll onto his side. A faint, night-cool breeze came in through the open window, chasing away some of his nausea. If he could just make it to the waste basket, retrieve his discarded Colt . . .

The sudden drum of approaching horses filtered into the room and a blade of tension sliced through him. Phipps stuck his head out the window and said something to the riders, who were almost certainly Paget, Rio and Casey. Then the safe-cracker turned to Barrow.

"All clear out there, Henry?"

"All clear," Barrow replied, closing the door again.

"All right. Best you plug up your ears, then."

He hustled back into the Englishman's office, fishing a lucifer out of his jacket pocket as he went. Luke strained to lift his head. Through a forest of desk- and chair-legs, he saw Phipps strike the match on the sole of one shoe and touch the flame to each of the three lengths of fuse. One by one they began to sputter and fizz like Fourth of July sparklers.

Again he tried to get his arms under him, to push up, reach across and into the waste basket, grab the .45 and start getting even.

Barney Phipps hustled out of the

Englishman's office and closed the door behind him. He went across to Barrow and they both hunkered down as far from the adjoining office wall as they could get.

Luke rolled onto his stomach. The effort just to get that far left him exhausted. He got his arms under him and started to drag himself towards the waste basket.

That's when the dynamite blew.

It went with a dull, violent thud and tore the door off the Englishman's office. They went temporarily deaf then, the lot of them, as grey smoke billowed out through the aperture and a wave of sticky, oven-heat washed over them. Then Phipps and Barrow were back on their feet and racing into the wreathing fog, hands waving before their coughing faces to clear the dusty air.

Luke's hearing came back with a pop that left him feeling sick again. He heard some shouting, the spooked, womanish neigh of frightened horses, the last dull echoes of the explosion as it sent its shock-waves into history.

The smoke began to thin and clear. He saw Phipps and Barrow transferring the contents of the shattered safe into the carpetbag. Again he fought to rise; he made it to his knees this time, as the ageing owlhoots burst back into the anteroom, threw the carpetbag to their waiting companions beyond the window, then made to follow it. Phipps went first, his movements surprisingly lithe. Then Barrow put his foot on the sill and began to hoist himself up.

Luke virtually threw himself at the waste basket. It fell onto its side and spilled the .45 onto the carpet. He snatched up the gun. Just feeling its cross-hatched walnut grips made him feel stronger.

"Barrow!"

Instinctively the lanky man froze for a moment, then spun around. Luke saw his eyes go wide an instant before he pulled the trigger.

The shot tore the smoky air apart

and gouged a chunk out of the window-frame to shower Barrow with splinters. At once he returned fire, but he was shooting wild and his slug embedded itself into the wall three feet above Luke's head.

Luke blasted at him again, but by then it was too late; Barrow was gone.

With a curse, he got his legs under him, but because they still felt like jelly, they melted pretty quick and he fell down again. He heard a series of yells and shouts coming in from beyond the window, followed by the sudden eruption of horses' hooves as the robbers dug in their heels and got their mounts moving.

He struggled back to his feet. Goddammit, he couldn't let them get away now! He made it over to the window just as another flurry of gunshots broke through the night, and he threw himself down fast. It was only when the window-frame failed to burst apart under the impact of so many slugs that he realised the outlaws had been shooting at something — or some*one* — else.

"What'n hell — ?"

As he struggled back to his full height, the ante-room door swung open and Jim Nodeen barrelled in with a Smith & Wesson .45 in his big, scarred fist. Behind him Luke saw a positive sea of faces, curious guests mostly, each one wearing a question mark for an expression.

Nodeen pulled up sharp. His piggy little eyes darted around the room, taking in the reek of smoke, the chaos, the sprawled form of John Colfax.

"Jesus Christ, what's been *happenin'* here?"

Luke shook his head to clear it some more. In a couple of terse sentences he answered the other man's question. Then he said, "You'd better get a doctor." He jabbed a finger at Colfax. "I don't know how badly they beat him."

"*Luke!*"

Mai shoved through the crowd then,

her oval face a picture of concern. She crossed the room at a run, her emerald green jacket and pants rasping a silken accompaniment to her movements. He caught her up in one arm and she buried her face in his shoulder. She was only small, but in that moment she very nearly squeezed all the wind out of him.

"Luke . . . " Looking up again, she ran her almond-shaped eyes over him, her expression one of such concern it was almost painful to behold. "You are all right? Your face . . . who *were* they? What did they do to you?"

There was some more gunfire. A few of the people in the hallway drew in their breath or ran for cover or screamed. Then all they could hear was the thud and roll of retreating hooves.

A wave of weakness washed over Luke but he fought it off. He stuffed his Colt back into leather and took the young Oriental girl by the arms. He could feel her trembling beneath his grip. "Don't worry about me, Mai. I'm all right. Just see what you can do for Colfax, will you? Until Nodeen fetches that doctor?"

Mai glanced over her shoulder. By the far wall, the Englishman was finally beginning to stir, his face screwed up, one hand going to his forehead.

"What about you?" she asked, turning back to face her lover. "You too have been beaten."

"I'll live," he replied. "But those sons were shooting at something out there just now. I'd better find out what it was."

He turned and climbed out through the window. It was a short drop to the now-trampled grass verge below. The night was star- and moon-bright. Yellow light from a hundred windows also helped illuminate the grounds.

There was a body sprawled out there, about seventy-five yards away.

Luke drew in the cool night air. It felt good after the stuffiness of the room. He palmed his Colt again and covered the distance at a run. The hotel, the surrounding hills, everything was eerily silent now, like the inside of a coffin. The robbery, the violence, it could have been a dream but for this vivid reminder of its awful reality.

He came to a halt beside the body. A groan that had nothing to do with his own hurts came out of him as he identified the bright red jacket and black pants edged with a yellow stripe.

It was one of the bell-hops.

It was Jess Monroe.

He shoved the handgun away and knelt beside the youngster. Blood sparkled on the kid's chest, on the line of it that threaded from his twisted lips. Luke glanced down at the boy's injuries. Near as he could see, Jess'd been shot more than once. In their getaway, the robbers had also run him down with their horses. He was broken, this boy, broken and dying.

"Who-who's . . . who's there?"

He cleared his throat. "Lay still, Jess."

"M-Mr Heller?"

Luke reached down and squeezed his shoulder lightly. "I'm here, son."

"I . . . I seen 'em, Mr Heller. Just after th-that explosion. They . . . they s-saw me, too, before I could get out of their way . . ."

"Easy, now." Luke glanced over his shoulder. "Get a doctor out here quickly!" he yelled to the figures now crowding the Englishman's office window.

The boy swallowed some of the blood that was rising in his throat. "I shot 'em," he said after a moment. It was only then that Luke saw moonlight reflecting on the octagonal barrel of the Colt Wells Fargo in the youngster's right hand. "Didn't do me no good, though, did it?"

"Just try to relax, son. Help's on its way."

"But I h-hurt awful bad, Mr Heller. An' . . . I'm awful scared."

Luke squeezed his shoulder again and looked back over his shoulder.

"For God's sake get a doctor out here!"

By the time he turned back to the boy, however, he was dead.

The speed of his passing hit the Tombstone detective like a fist in the guts. He sagged, moaned softly, his faith in human nature somehow tarnished by the death of this young man.

Then his face hardened.

He climbed quickly to his feet, his green eyes fixed on the darkness into which Phipps, Barrow and the others had ridden.

There'd be time enough for mourning later. Right now there was only time for revenge.

7

LUKE went around to the front of the building and up the steps into the lobby feeling tired and sore and hollow.

Hotel employees were bustling about all over the place. Guests had congregated into little knots and were busy speculating on this new turn of events. Luke ignored them all. He made it to the desk and called Prissy across to him. The clerk came over, obviously agitated by news of the robbery.

"Mr Heller! My goodness, they're saying those miscreants beat you to within an inch of your life, sir, and then stole forty thousand dollars!"

The man from Tombstone cleared his throat. He looked like hell and he felt pretty much how he looked. "There's a boy on the lawn out back," he said in a flat voice. "Jess Monroe. You know him?"

Prissy nodded slowly. "I know *of* him."

"He's dead. They killed him."

"Oh, no!"

"I want you to have a couple fellers take him to the icehouse and then get a mortician up here to take proper care of him."

The desk-clerk nodded, shock leeching the blood from his face. "I'll attend to it at once."

"Obliged. You heard how Colfax is?"

"I believe he will be all right, Mr Heller. A slight concussion, a few bruised ribs, but nothing more serious than that."

"Have you sent for the local law?"

"Marshal Ward has been summoned, yes."

Luke nodded. "All right. Get someone to rig out my horse, will you? It's the coffee-coloured gelding with the bad temper. They'll find my rig on the saddle tree, it's a Denver."

"You're not going after them, surely?"

"I'm gonna do more than that. I'm gonna bring 'em back — *in* their saddles or *over* 'em."

Prissy eyed him closely. "Is that wise, do you think?"

"Just see to it."

He turned away from the desk and headed for the stairs. He had to move fast, before the robbers put too much distance between them. He took the stairs two at a time, but as he reached his room, he saw that Mai was already there, packing his saddlebags.

"You are going after them," she said simply.

He closed the door behind him, peeled off his jacket, shoulder-rig, vest and shirt. "Uh-huh." He went across to the bowl on the dresser, filled it with cold water and quickly washed his battered face.

"I have packed everything you are likely to need," the Chinese girl said as he towelled himself dry, then sat on the end of the bed, pulled off his town shoes and took off his pants. "There is fresh water in your canteen, food in your saddlebags, spare ammunition for your weapons."

He looked up at her. He knew how much it had cost her to help him like this instead of begging him to stay and leave it all to the authorities. Not for the first time he realised that he'd found a partner and a half in this sweet-natured, sensitive young woman.

He said, "Thanks, Mai."

He got up and went to the dresser, where he hurriedly chose some fresh clothes, a striped cotton shirt and sturdy brown wool pants. He pulled on low stovepipe boots and strapped his tooled black leather gunbelt about his hips, then transferred the Frontier Colt from the shoulder-rig to the holster.

At last he shrugged into a fringed buckskin jacket and placed a battered brown Stetson on his head. Then he came across and pulled her to him.

"Oh, Luke," she said, burying her

head in his chest so that her soft, high voice was muffled by his shirt. "What is happening here? Murder, robbery . . . I did not *dream* it would be like this."

"Me neither," he said grimly.

"*Xiaoxin*," she whispered, so distracted by worry for him that she momentarily reverted to her own language. "Be careful, Luke."

"I will."

Gently he detached himself from her, grabbed up his saddlebags and sheathed Winchester .44/40 and went to the door. Her voice stopped him there.

"Luke."

"Yeah?"

She forced a brave, quivery little smile. "I love you."

He looked at her, his square, rugged face immobile. He'd never heard her say those words before. It had been a long time since he'd heard them from *anyone*.

He said, "I love you, too."

Then he left the room.

* * *

As he reached the foot of the stairs, Prissy called across to him. "A word if I may, Mr Heller."

"Sure, but make it quick."

As he reached the desk, Prissy said confidentially, "A few of the men, the guides, hunters and labourers, have asked if they might accompany you on your quest."

"Thanks, but no thanks. I appreciate the offer, but I'll make better time on my own."

"Are you sure?"

"I'm sure."

Prissy shrugged. "Very well. One of the boys has got your horse out front, Mr Heller. Good luck to you."

Luke nodded. "Thanks."

He hurried out into the faintly-lit darkness. It was approaching midnight now. One day was dying, another was in the wings just waiting to be born. Down on the gravel drive, one of the bell-hops was rubbing at his ornery gelding's head, and the horse was loving every minute of it. A few yards away, Anthony Brandon was sitting astride a distinctive blaze-faced charcoal mare. The New York attorney was dressed in dark brown corduroys, a tan workshirt, sheepskin coat and riding boots. Luke saw a gunbelt strapped around the man's hips, the butt of Brandon's New Line Police Colt projecting from the holster. Through the gloom he also saw the stock of a repeating rifle sticking up from the man's saddle.

As he set about buckling his saddlebags behind his cantle, the man from Tombstone said, "Kind of late to be going for a ride, isn't it?"

The handsome man only shrugged. "I'm coming with you, Mr Heller."

Luke worked swiftly, by touch. "No you're not."

"You're a fool if you think you can handle five-to-one odds," the lawyer pointed out reasonably but firmly. "And I don't think you're a fool, Mr Heller."

Luke fixed his Winchester to the Denver rig's offside, then took the reins from the boy and dismissed him with a nod of thanks. For once Goddam made no attempt to bite or otherwise savage his master. Perhaps even he sensed that this was not the time for such shenanigans.

"Am I missing the point here, Brandon?" Luke asked as he toed into leather and swung astride the gelding. "You're a lawyer, aren't you? This isn't your fight. Neither is it a game. One kid has already died tonight. If you think this business has been laid on just so you can enjoy the excitement of a real live manhunt, you can forget it."

"I'm not in this for the thrill of it, I can promise you that," Brandon replied, getting angry now. "We have enough murder and mayhem back East as well, you know."

"Then why *do* you want to buy into this?"

"Because you've been kind to Mrs Cameron . . . Juliet . . . and I'd like to help. Besides, it's entirely possible that one of the men you're after could have also been responsible for Austin's death."

That was a turn-up, Luke thought. But wouldn't it make sense for a killer to go out hunting some *other* killers as a means of diverting suspicion from himself? It would be if he was a clever man, used to thinking in devious ways the way attornies thought, maybe.

Or perhaps there was another reason for Brandon's offer. Perhaps he'd found some evidence, something left out of place, maybe, that Luke had been through his room. The gun, the letter from Juliet Cameron . . . they could be damning evidence. Out on the trail of the robbers, Brandon could dispatch Luke without anyone being the wiser, and blame *his* death on the outlaws, too.

He heaved a sigh. "All right, Brandon. I don't have time to argue, and I see that you're dressed for the trail, so let's get moving." He eyed the Easterner closely. "You *can* ride, I assume?"

"Yes."

"And use those weapons?"

"Proficiently enough."

"Where'd you get them, anyway?"

"The handgun's my own. I borrowed the rifle from one of the hunters."

They moved out, tearing up a spray of gravel first, then great chunks of turf as Luke led them on a course around back of the hotel, where he had last seen the robbers disappearing into the darkness. There he reined down and sat his saddle for a moment, thinking.

"Well?" asked Brandon.

Luke considered. Part of his mind had been doing just that ever since the robbery, of course. He'd looked at it from every angle, and always came back to the same conclusion. Phipps and Barrow, they were old hands at this game. They'd have worked everything out to the last detail including a fast exit from these mountains. An exit most likely provided by the railroad.

"So you're saying they've headed for

Grey Springs," the handsome lawyer said after Luke voiced his thoughts.

Luke shook his head. "I doubt it. If they went that way, they'd run the risk of crossing trails with Ward, the local lawman."

"Then what's the alternative?"

"A little town about twenty five miles west of here called Haynesville. The rails run right through there."

"But surely, Grey Springs is nearer?"

Luke glanced at him. "I don't have time to argue with you, Brandon. Come with me to Haynesville or go to Grey Springs by yourself."

"There's no need to take that tone. All right. You know the way these killers are likely to think. We'll do it your way."

"So what are we waiting for?" Luke shot back. "Let's ride!"

★ ★ ★

The first grey promise of dawn was slowly lightening the eastern horizon when Luke and Brandon topped a rise, drew down and saw Haynesville set out below them.

Luke rubbed at his gritty eyes while Brandon eased his spine out straight. It had been a long, cheerless night and the pace had been as gruelling as they could safely make it. But there'd been spots along the trail where they'd had to slow their mounts to a walk for fear of running them into trees or rabbit-holes, and soon the handicap the darkness represented had grown as irksome as hell.

They'd stuck with it, though. They *had* to. The trail had worn on. It dipped and rose, ran arrow-straight, then twisted like a cottonmouth. Timber rose thick and shadowy on more than one occasion, ambush country, and they'd had to slow down to negotiate that safely, too.

Now, as they topped out and spied a meagre scattering of saffron lights somewhere below, the man from Tombstone exchanged a glance with his unlikely companion and without a word they kicked their horses back to speed, hoping like hell that Luke's guess had been right, that Phipps and Barrow and the others *had* decided to pick up the night-train here, that this little mountain town would mark the end of the chase, and a time of reckoning.

As they closed the distance to the town limits, Luke thought he could detect the smoky, oily scent of a locomotive on the pre-dawn air. Brandon must have caught it too, because suddenly the pair of them were fighting to get one last burst of speed from their horses.

Suddenly the ground beneath them flattened out. Rounding a bend in the trail, the two men spied a mean little rail depot just this side of the town, with a train waiting outside the station house. The place was maybe two, three hundred yards distant.

Wind slipped past their faces. They had to narrow their eyes down to slits.

Grass gave way to hardpan. Clapboard dwellings rose up, each one separated from its neighbour by a shadow-infested dog-trot.

Up ahead, the locomotive was belching grey steam from someplace between its large, metallic wheels. Luke saw it quite clearly now, a man-made snake; the loco, tender, day-cars, club car, caboose.

A voice cut through the slowly-lightening day. *"Board! Final call! All aboard!"*

The thunder of their horses' hooves was deafening as they angled their mounts in a wide sweep that took them around back of the caboose. Luke edged out ahead of the attorney. He sent Goddam leaping across the gleaming tracks and reined in at the far, sloping end of the weathered platform.

He was looping Goddam's reins around a low picket fence there as Brandon brought his rented charcoal to a wild, dust-raising halt alongside him. Luke flung an order at him even as the handsome man dismounted.

"Go take a quick look around out front, but hurry! That train's just about to leave!"

Brandon nodded. "What about you?"

"I'll tackle the stationmaster!"

They split up. Luke clattered up the ramp and onto the platform. There wasn't much to see, and what there was was illuminated only by two storm lanterns, one hanging at each end of the overhead awning.

The stationmaster, up by the engine, was just waving to the conductor, who was leaning out from the caboose platform, one hand gripping the iron rail there, the other waving back.

Up front, the air was ripped apart by the train's shrill whistle.

Spewing steam, the train began to inch sluggishly forward.

The stationmaster spotted him then, and started down the platform towards him. A faint breeze made the lanterns sway lazily. Shadows danced on the depot walls. Luke, meanwhile, broke into a trot, one eye on the darkened carriage windows as the train slowly picked up speed.

At last the stationmaster was near enough to ask him what he wanted. "You're a little late if you wuz hopin' to catch the train."

Just as Luke opened his mouth to speak, Brandon's voice tore across the huff, puff and groan of the moving train.

"*Heller!*"

Luke spun as Brandon came up onto the platform at a run.

"Five horses tied up at the hitch-rack out front!" he yelled. "Ridden hard, by the looks of them!"

Luke turned back to the stationmaster. "Five men," he said urgently. "They just buy passage aboard that train?"

The stationmaster, who was getting along in years, looked thoroughly bewildered and not a little suspicious. "Well, now . . . "

"Yes or no?" snapped Luke.

A lifetime spent obeying orders made

the stationmaster respond at once. "Yes!"

Luke's reaction was no less swift. "All right; look after our horses, mister. We'll be back for 'em! Come on, Brandon — we've got a train to catch!"

He ran for the rapidly-departing string of coaches with Brandon right behind him, came level with the swaying caboose, reached out, grabbed the cold iron rail and swung himself aboard. The train picked up speed with a sudden lurch that nearly threw him off the other side of the narrow platform as Brandon, still pumping along beside the train, grabbed for the rail and missed. For a moment, Luke thought the lawyer's legs were going to go out from under him, but somehow he kept going, tried again, missed again —

Luke reached out, grasped him by one wrist, braced himself more firmly, reached down with the other hand. Brandon grabbed hold, nodded, and Luke hauled him forward just as the train went around a bend and spruce-speckled slopes closed them in on both sides.

Brandon's legs swung out wildly, and then he came up onto the platform. As the train began to climb a gradient, both men were tossed around like so much flotsam. At last they found their balance, each man breathing like a blacksmith's bellows, sweating hard but relieved not to have missed the train.

"You . . . you all right?" Luke asked after a moment.

Brandon nodded. "Yes . . . thanks to you."

"Come . . . come on, then. Let's see what we can do about finding the men we're after."

They turned around just as the caboose door swung open and they came eyeball-on first to the dark barrel of a .476-calibre Enfield Mark I revolver, then to the mad-looking man who was holding it on them.

★ ★ ★

The man who'd got the drop on them had to shout to make himself heard above all the clanking and rattling.

"All right, now, that's far enough! Just who are you, eh? An' what do you think you're doin' boardin' my train in such an uncivilised manner?"

Luke and Brandon exchanged a look filled with relief. For one moment there the man from Tombstone thought they'd met up with their quarry a little earlier than planned. Now, as the newcomer stepped through the doorway and onto the wind-whipped platform, they saw his uniform in the building dawn-light and identified him as the captain of the train.

"It's a long story, friend, and we can't spare the time to tell it," Luke replied in as reasonable a tone as he could manage.

The conductor wig-waggled the Enfield Mark I. "I think you'd *better* find the time to tell it! And keep your hands up, the pair of you!"

Brandon took it upon himself to reply

as he raised his smooth, manicured hands higher. "You've heard of the Mountain View Hotel?" he asked.

"O' course."

"It was robbed earlier tonight . . . that is to say, *last* night. And the robbers are on this train."

The conductor's eyes narrowed suspiciously. "That sounds a likely story."

"It's true. The five men who boarded the train back at Haynesville — "

Luke bought into it again. Cracking the whip had worked with the stationmaster; maybe it would also turn the trick with the conductor. "Listen, mister; it's like I said just now. We haven't got the time for this. You'll just have to take our word for it. The robbers are on this train, and we're here to take them back."

"You're the law?" the conductor asked warily.

"I'm security at the hotel," Luke replied. "This here's my assistant."

"You got some identification to that effect?"

"Sure."

Luke lowered his left hand first, and while the conductor's rheumy eyes were following that, his right dropped down fast and came up again filled with Colt.

"Not a move nor a sound," he said as he took the revolver from the other man and passed it to Brandon. "Unload it."

The conductor, meanwhile, looked mad enough to chew nails and spit rust. "Why, you — "

"Not a sound, I said," Luke reminded him. "Now turn around and get back inside. And remember this, mister. We're on your side. We mean you no harm. But try to cross me now and I won't think twice about cold-cocking you."

They went into the dark, cluttered caboose with the conductor still muttering indignantly. When Brandon gave the empty gun back to him, he calmed down a little.

"Now, these five men we're after," Luke began. "You must've seen 'em. They likely boarded the train as soon as it pulled in at Haynesville."

"They did."

"Where'd they sit?"

The conductor held back a moment. "They *really* robbers?" he asked.

"Uh-huh."

"All right. Centre carriage. Up front."

"Facing this way?"

"Facin' the engine."

"You'd better be damned sure of yourself, mister."

"I am, don't fret." The conductor looked from Luke to Brandon. "Well, what you waitin' for? I'm sure as hell not gonna stop you, am I? All I ask is one thing . . ."

"What?"

"Watch out for my other passengers, will you? They got a right to travel these rails in safety, you know."

Grimly Luke strode the length of

the caboose and opened the far door. Brandon was right behind him as he hopped from one swaying wrought-iron platform to the next. And that's what worried him; having Brandon behind him.

He paused a moment and glanced back at his partner. Brandon had already drawn his .38. But for what purpose? Was he simply preparing for the coming confrontation, or getting ready to put a bullet in Luke's spine?

The attorney's face was tight and unreadable. It was a courtroom face, a face that gave nothing away.

But hell, maybe there was nothing *to* give away. Maybe Luke was getting just a little too jumpy. After all, he didn't even know for sure if Brandon had been involved in Austin Cameron's murder, much less whether or not he was plotting Luke's demise, too.

Slowly Luke faced front again and let himself into the club car.

At this early hour, the car was empty. He'd suspected as much, but his guts had still wound tighter than a Swiss watch as he made his entrance.

Brandon followed him inside and closed the door behind him. The loud, rough sounds of travel were immediately muted. The coach rolled along with a gentle rocking motion that made the cutlery and up-turned glasses on the tables clink or rattle softly. Beyond the windows, the mountains flew past in all their green splendour. Trees streamed by, a few of the longer branches tapping at the glass and dragging along the carriage's outer wall. Then the view changed. Rolling hills stippled with wild flowers swelled up towards a distant sky that was now blue-grey.

The two men worked their way up the carriage to the far door. If Brandon meant him some harm, he'd never get a better chance than now to inflict it. But they reached their destination without event, and as Luke stepped out onto the next platform, he allowed himself to relax for just a moment.

The next car into which he stepped was a passenger car. The dark-wood walls gave it a gloomy aspect that a veritable shroud of stale cigarette, cigar and pipe-smoke hovering around the ceiling did nothing to dispell. The aisle was narrow and littery. Row upon row of upholstered seats shelved ahead. Most of the passengers — rangemen, drummers, women of all ages, many cradling babies or young children — were still trying to doze despite the best efforts of the train to shake them awake.

Luke moved forward cautiously. If the conductor was right, if the robbers hadn't changed places for some reason after the train pulled out, he would find them in the next carriage.

He glanced down into the faces of the people he passed. They worried him. He wanted to handle this business as quickly and cleanly as he could. Like the conductor, he had no wish to involve innocent bystanders in a shootout. But what about the men he was after? He had no doubt that Phipps and the rest would turn this train into a bloodbath if doing so meant the difference between escape and capture — and a bloodbath was something he dearly wished to avoid.

The train lurched around a sharp mountain curve and Luke reached out to steady himself with one hand, trying to keep his gun down at his side, out of sight, to avoid panicking the slowly-stirring passengers, Brandon following his example.

They let themselves out onto the next platform.

"Watch your step!" Luke shouted above the rush of wind and the train's accompanying clank-clank roar as he leapt across to the next passenger car. Brandon followed him without comment, his face showing signs of tension now, a tension that was forcing some of the tiredness from his glassy eyes.

Jerking open the door, they entered the next carriage. It was virtually a carbon-copy of the first. Growing sunlight fell in through the eastern-facing windows like dust-filled gold bars, illuminating sluggish-but-shifting passengers of both sexes and all ages.

Luke pulled up so sharp that Brandon very nearly blundered into him. Without a word, the Tombstone detective raised his left hand and pointed towards the front of the carriage, where the heads of their quarry could just be seen above the seat-backs.

Luke pulled down a deep breath that steadied him against a heady rush of adrenalin, then started forward. He hadn't gone more than a few paces when a woman in a poke bonnet saw the Frontier Colt in his fist, mistook him for a road agent and let loose a scream that tore through the stuffy air.

At once the carriage came to life as panic hit everyone around them like a flash-flood. Babies and young children began to howl. Other women strained their lungs. Men began to yell even though they didn't properly know yet what they were yelling for.

And up at the far end of the carriage, the men Luke and Brandon had been hoping to brace with the minimum of fuss twisted around to face them.

"Dammit!"

Recognition hit them all in that one heart-stopping moment. Henry Barrow's eyes went widest of all, and he yelled Luke's name as he came up out of his seat — and clawed for his gun.

8

THERE was no time for Luke to curse his bad luck, even if cursing it would have made him feel any better about the mess he'd somehow walked into, so he didn't waste his time on any of that, he just allowed his instincts to take over, and levelling his .45 he fixed the robbers with a glare and yelled, "Hands up, the lot of you! I mean it — hands *up*!"

He knew they had no intention of giving up without a fight, though, and he didn't have to wait long to have his suspicions confirmed.

Henry Barrow swung his Smith & Wesson Schofield up and thumbed back the hammer to trigger the first shot of the conflict.

Luke beat him to it.

The Frontier Colt bucked against his palm and the thunder of the blast awoke a fresh cacophony of yelling and screaming from the people around him, most of whom immediately threw themselves to the floor.

As one of the outlaws went down behind the cover of their seats, though what they didn't know right then was that Luke was deliberately aiming high. There were too many innocent people in the way for him to risk shooting any lower, and his first duty was to them. As much as he wanted to collar the fleeing robbers, he had a responsibility to make sure these bystanders came to no harm.

The robbers had no such compunctions, though, and Paget, the man with the white-blond hair, came around his seat with a Peacemaker blazing in his fist. Luke shoved Brandon aside and threw himself down onto the worn aisle covering just as Paget's bullets shattered glass and buzzed the length of the rocking carriage like angry hornets.

Now Luke didn't know what was more deafening, the crash of gunfire or the bawling of the frightened passengers. He returned fire, his bullet gouging another yellow-white scar out of the wood panelling behind the robbers, again just trying to keep the outlaws down, to stop the situation from going from bad to worse.

Rio came up then, working an Adams .442. Luke rolled, came up in a crouch between one row of seats and the next, alongside an elderly man and a young, shivering woman, just as lead sliced the smoke-tinged air.

He glanced across at Brandon. The attorney looked pale and nauseous. Then he heard footsteps and swore.

Thumbing back the Colt's hammer, he waited a couple of heartbeats, then chanced a look around the seat.

The door at the far end of the carriage was swinging slowly back and forth to the movement of the train. There was no longer any sign of the robbers.

"Damn!"

Luke powered up out of his crouch and took the aisle at a sprint. He felt awful, for the long ride and subsequent rigours had done little to help his punished muscles recuperate from their earlier beating. Still, there'd be time for rest later, with luck. Right now, all that mattered was catching up with the men who'd killed Jess Monroe — and praying that it wouldn't occur to the sonsofbitches to take hostages on their way through the next carriage.

Brandon joined Luke in his race for the still-swinging door, but they were forced to drop to the floor again as Rio, just about to disappear through the portal leading to the next carriage, turned to get off two last shots.

Quickly Luke climbed back to his feet just in time to return fire as the dark-skinned halfbreed turned away. A crimson spray erupted from Rio's spine as he fell forward through the opening into the car ahead. Then two more shots boomed out and lead slammed into the doorway near Luke's head, forcing him to crouch once more.

"We've got them on the run!" Brandon announced.

"Maybe," Luke replied, not entirely convinced. "You all right, Brandon?"

The New Yorker nodded.

"You look a little grey to me."

"Just . . . reaction, that's all. I'm not used to this. But I'll live."

They waited a moment, the screams still echoing behind them now mingling with the panicky yelps coming from up ahead. Then they jumped through the doorway and stormed across into the next car. Anticipating shots, they crouched low upon entering, but no shots rang out. Neither did there appear to be any sign of the men they were after.

People were huddling down between their seats. A few of the women and nearly all of the children were crying. Some of the braver men shouted questions, demanding to know what was going on. Luke and Brandon ignored them.

The aisle was blocked by the body of the man Luke had just shot. They gave him a cursory examination. Rio's back was a mess. It was impossible to imagine he could live through such a wound.

"One down," Brandon said grimly.

Luke had never been a one to keep score, but as he made to reply, he heard a clank and screech, followed by a metallic groan that came from outside the car ahead of them. Almost immediately Luke guessed what had happened as he and Brandon ran towards the door at the far end of the car. The lawyer beat him there by seconds.

"My God! Heller — they've uncoupled the train!"

It was true. The car Luke and Brandon were standing in was slowing down while the remainder of the train — the loco and tender — was continuing to pull rapidly away. Casey, the fat bald man who'd given Luke such a beating, was balancing awkwardly up on the tender. Impulsively Brandon raised his pistol and got off two shots that sent the outlaw scrambling to the far side of the piled coal. A few hasty return shots crashed through the air and Luke and Brandon were forced back into the carriage as the tail-end of the train slowed still further and the gap between the hunters and the hunted widened.

For just a moment Luke felt defeat weigh heavily upon him. His lips tightened in a mixture of fury and annoyance. The loco steamed on up the track, pulling away still further as it belched black clouds from its brightly-painted stack to stain the otherwise clear, early-morning air. Soon it barrelled around a bend and was lost to sight.

"What do we do *now*?" asked Brandon. When no reply was forthcoming he said, "Did you hear me, Heller? I said — "

"I heard you," Luke cut in, going back out onto the platform to turn the big iron wheel that would brake the remaining carriages to a stop.

"Then what do we do now?" the attorney asked. "It looks as if they've out-foxed us."

"Not yet they haven't."

"But they'll be half-way to the next town down the line by now, and we have no way of giving chase."

"I'm hoping we can pick up a couple of horses just over on that next hill."

Brandon looked in the direction Luke indicated with a nod and saw a small farmhouse a little over a mile in the distance.

Behind them, the train was now in uproar. Some of the male passengers had had enough of cowering and were beginning to look as if they were going to take the law into their own hands. It was time to move on.

They hopped down from the car and set out across the gently-sloping field. By the time someone ventured out onto the platform and yelled for them to come on back and answer some questions, they were a quarter-mile away and still going.

They reached the dwelling, a sturdy log structure and out-buildings that looked both clean and comfortable, within half an hour. A man was working out front, chopping wood with a big double-bladed axe. He was a tall fellow, about six feet four, and he weighed in at around two hundred-forty-odd pounds. The grey streaks in his hair and beard put him somewhere in his forties. Now he offered the new arrivals a guarded welcome while keeping a firm grip on the axe resting across his right shoulder.

"Mornin'. You fellers've had a little trouble with your train, I see."

"Uh-huh," Luke replied. "That's why I was hoping we could trouble you for the loan of a couple of horses."

The man's blue eyes narrowed. "Well now," he replied. "That depends. Who are you, and what's your business?"

There was no time for any of that. Brandon knew it as well as Luke, and quickly stepped forward to take command. "You *do* have some horses for sale or rent, then?" he asked.

"Sure."

Brandon took out his wallet. "Then we'll rent them, no questions asked, for one hundred dollars."

He produced a C-note and the farmer's eyes came out on stalks.

"You got it," he said, coming forward to fold his free hand around the bill. Glancing over towards the cabin, he added, "It's okay, honey. These fellers is friends."

The men from the Mountain View shifted their gaze that way and were just in time to see a rifle muzzle being withdrawn from one of the tarpaper windows out front.

"How 'bout a cup of coffee while I rig out the horses?" asked the farmer sociably.

There was no denying that coffee would come awful welcome about then, and drive away some of the tension still knotting both mens' innards, but time was against them. "No thanks," Luke said regretfully. "But if you could put a couple of eats in a bag for us . . ."

"Sure," the man replied. "My wife'll fix up some biscuits and preserves for you while I saddle up."

As the big farmer set down his axe and hustled away to fetch the horses, Luke rubbed tiredly at his eyes, then studied Brandon's profile. "I'll see to it that you get that money back," he promised.

The attorney shrugged. "There's time enough for that."

Luke frowned. It wasn't exactly the best time he could have chosen to pursue the subject, but he was curious. "Tell me, Brandon. Just what is your relationship with Mrs Cameron?"

Brandon was surprised by the question. "I thought we'd already been over that."

"Refresh my memory."

Brandon's face tightened a little. "I was Austin's lawyer," he said at length. "A friend of the family."

Luke eyed him directly. "Nothing more than that?" he prodded.

Now the attorney bristled. "Just what's that supposed to mean?"

"What do you think it means? I've seen you with Mrs Cameron. I'd say you were more than just a family friend. I'm right, aren't I?"

Brandon sighed. The day was starting to warm up, and birds were singing in the distant trees. It was peaceful in the yard, a universe away from the violence they'd so recently encountered on the train.

"Yes, you're right," Brandon said after a while. "But you're wrong as well, Heller. It's not how you think it is. Juliet and I have known each other for years. We grew up together back in Pennsylvania. In fact, it was Juliet who talked Austin into putting his bank's business my way after the two of them got married a few years ago.

Luke said, "So where's the harm in that?"

"There isn't any."

"And yet you tried to keep it quiet."

"I guess I thought . . . well, to be candid, I suppose I thought someone like you might jump to the wrong conclusion if you knew she and I had once had . . . an understanding."

"Were you in love with her, Brandon?"

The lawyer thought about that. "Years ago," he said at length.

"Why didn't you marry her? Wouldn't she have you?"

"At that time she deserved far more than I could hope to give her. God, when I was working my way through law school, it was as much as I could do just to support *myself*. But I owe Juliet a lot. As I said, we're old friends. And I know exactly what you're trying to imply, Heller, and I don't appreciate your vulgar insinuations."

"Okay," Luke replied, smiling tiredly to diffuse the situation. "But you'll appreciate that I had to ask."

The farmer came back across the yard leading two saddled horses, a little paint pony he called Missy and a fine, sturdy stallion by the name of Sampson. "They ain't the finest horses you'll ever ride, but they got bottom and they'll give you no nonsense," he declared, handing over the reins. "Just leave 'em at Fordyce's Livery in Blair Town when you're through with 'em. My wife's put your eats in that burlap bag around the saddlehorn."

"Thanks." Luke glanced around. "If we can just trouble you for some directions to this place, Blair Town . . ."

The farmer pointed towards a narrow dirt path that wound off into the trees and hills about three hundred yards northeast. "Take that trail there. It'll cut quite a few miles off the distance your train'd have to travel to get through these mountains. 'Fact, I figger that you fellers could just about catch *up* with that train iffen you hustle."

Luke and Brandon swung up into borrowed saddles. "Thanks, mister."

They spurred the horses to a steady gallop off down the trail to the next town. Taking the lead, Luke considered his conversation with the young lawyer. He'd certainly sounded sincere. But then, lawyers could be mighty plausible when it suited them, and try as he might, he couldn't shake his suspicions about the other man.

Still, Brandon seemed to be an honest sort, near as he could judge. Furthermore, if Brandon was aware of Luke's suspicions and wanted to eliminate him, there'd been enough opportunities for him to make his move before this. Was he still trying to pluck up enough nerve for it?

Luke just didn't know.

At some time around noon, the warm air was suddenly shattered by a series of distant gun-blasts. The two men exchanged a grim glance, then urged their animals to greater speed. They emerged from the forest aboard two near-beat horses six or seven minutes later and saw Blair Town set out before them. It wasn't much more than a collection of cabins, some houses, a general store, a stable with a blacksmith's shop and a small station house that served the railroad that passed through the community.

"There it is, Luke!" said Brandon wearily. "We made it!"

A jolt of expectation washed through the man from Tombstone. Yeah, they'd made it. And as he'd half-expected from those gunshots, the loco Phipps and the others had commandeered had only just pulled in at the depot itself!

A familiar tingle stirred the dark hairs at the nape of Luke's neck. Intuitively the detective could sense a fresh promise of danger and death in the mountain air.

Hauling iron, they sent the tired horses out onto the flats in one final gallop and brought them to a stop before the station house. The shaky firecrew were being questioned by an equally pale-faced station agent. Around them, townsfolk had gathered in a frightened knot. A murmur ran through them when they saw the newcomers, and Luke raised his gunhand quickly in greeting, before some keyed-up towner could grow trigger-happy.

"What happened?" Luke asked the station agent as he hipped the rented horse up alongside the hissing loco.

The station agent eyed him suspiciously. "An' jest who're you?"

Luke told him, condensing it all as much as he could.

The station agent and the rest of the men and women gathered around him listened in silence. Then the railroad official said, "Well, I'll have to take your word for it, I guess. But you're right; there *were* four bandits aboard the train, and they uncoupled the rollin' stock jest like you said. Held these here men at gunpoint — "

"Yeah, yeah; but where did they go after the train pulled in?"

"They leapt down an' ran off towards the north side of town, firin' revolvers at anythin' that moved," said the train driver.

"You got any idea where they could've been headed?"

The townsfolk pondered that. After a moment one of them said, "The ferry's out that way!"

Without a word, Luke turned his heaving horse around in a wide, dust-spiralling circle. "Come on, Brandon, let's pick up the trail!"

They angled their lathered mounts around the depot and onto the main drag just as a man wearing the shield of town constable came puffing up, yelling, "Hey there! You men! Hold up, I say!"

They paid him no mind. Instead they forced even greater speed from the horses, though Luke took no pleasure from pushing them like that. Still, he had no choice in the matter, not if he wanted to catch up with Jesse Monroe's killers. One thing was certain, though; the animals really *did* have bottom, just as the farmer they'd rented them from had promised.

The street was rutted hardpan. It

stretched ahead like a length of brown corduroy. They whipped past all the still-stalled traffic, ignoring all the yelled questions and curious stares they received along the way, aiming for the river on the far side of town, just visible now as a silver thread catching midday sunlight in its ripples and throwing them back skyward as winking white lights.

They were about halfway down the street when more gunfire split the silence, and somewhere up ahead a woman started screaming.

Movement caught their attention. Three men had just burst out of the little general store on the right-hand side of the street with guns drawn. The fourth was already on the boardwalk, keeping watch. Spying Heller and Brandon, the look-out — his short, fat build identifying him clearly as Casey — spun to face them. He had a pistol of some indeterminate make in his hand and the thing roared twice. Brandon returned fire but missed. Luke, who'd had more experience at this kind of fighting, reined down, turned his horse sideways-on to the man and fired his own Colt twice in response.

The slugs knocked Casey off the boardwalk and into the street. They appeared to have caved in his chest. As Brandon also reined to a halt, Casey's little legs began to drum a death-dance on the hardpan.

Barney Phipps, Henry Barrow and Paget stood momentarily frozen, the proceeds of their impromptu robbery — supplies for what was left of their journey to freedom — still clasped in their arms.

Then the spell was broken and they scrambled for cover. Since that was the wisest course to take, Luke and Brandon followed their example.

The street came alive with gunfire as the men from the Mountain View kicked free of their stirrups, threw themselves to earth and came up behind a trough fashioned from a hollowed-out tree-trunk that was situated just out front of the public corral.

"What now?" asked Brandon.

Careful to keep his head down, Luke surveyed their surroundings. "We need to get around behind 'em. That means working our way around back of this block. Still game, Brandon?"

A bullet struck the far side of the trough with a solid whack. "Still game," the attorney replied grimly.

Before they could make a move, however, someone on the other side of the street yelled, "They're makin' a run for it!"

Scooping off his Stetson, Luke chanced a look around the edge of the trough. Damn! It was true; the robbers *were* making a break for it, tearing across the street with their guns still blasting until they disappeared down a garbage-strewn dog-trot that must inevitably lead them closer to the river, the ferry — and escape.

"Let's move!" Luke yelled, and together he and the New Yorker threw caution aside and came up and around the trough to continue pursuit.

The street was deserted now, save for a positive caravan of hastily-abandoned wagons jamming the thoroughfare. As they sprinted from one piece of cover to the next, Luke and Brandon kept as low as they could, although neither man expected to meet much in the way of resistance now. They came up beside a stalled wagon, its two-horse team sidestepping in the traces, heads held high, eye-whites showing, and pulled down a fresh breath before setting off again.

They reached the mouth of the dog-trot just in time to see their quarry vanishing around the corner at its far end. Paget turned back once, his hat flying off to reveal his white-blond hair, and emptied what was left in his Peacemaker at them before racing on out of sight. Neither of his pursuers bothered to return fire.

The alleyway was narrow, cool in shadow, and stank of rotting trash. They thundered down it as fast as they dared, slowed as they reached the far end, and Brandon fell back a little while Luke edged ahead, keeping his back to the west wall until he could peer around the corner.

The dog-trot opened out into a backlot. Scrubby yellow-green grass swayed gently in a sudden cooling breeze. Luke went down on one knee to study the terrain ahead better. The weathered shell of a long-disused wagon sat up on blocks about sixty feet away, home now to rodents or nesting birds. About forty yards beyond that, built precariously close to the river that flowed sluggishly along behind it, stood a worn-out one-room shack, its windows dark and dusty, some of them jagged-edged and broken.

He hunkered there, using his eyes and ears, for a long moment. There was no sign of the robbers. It was as if the ground had opened up to swallow them.

Then Brandon's voice came as a

sibilant whisper close to his ear. "Heller — !"

"I see it."

About half-way between the alley-mouth and the wrecked wagon lay the carpetbag Phipps and Barrow had used to carry the money they'd stolen from the hotel safe. But had the thieves dropped the loot accidentally in their haste to get away, or deliberately, as a means of drawing Luke and Brandon out into the open where they could pick them off that much easier?

"Where do you suppose they are?" whispered the lawyer.

Luke took another pan across the backlot. There was no sound save the occasional soughing of the faint breeze and one or two yells from behind them as Blair Town tried to organise itself against all the chaos that had come to call.

"Not sure," he replied after a while. Without taking his eyes off the cabin, he reached down and scooped up Paget's fallen hat, held back a moment, then spun it high into the air, where it twisted in an arc and came back to earth somewhere near the carpetbag.

Luke had prepared himself for a sudden volley of gunblasts, but the movement attracted nothing, from the old shack or anyplace else.

He didn't quite know what to read into that. "Cover me," he said softly over his shoulder.

"Where — ?"

But Luke was already moving, and as he burst out of the dog-trot and covered the distance to the carpetbag at a lope, Brandon raised his .38 and fired two shots towards the cabin, to keep whoever might be in there otherwise occupied.

Luke reached down, grabbed up the bag and kept going. A moment later he went down behind the wagon, his boot-heels kicking up clods of earth as he came to a halt.

Again, there was no return fire, either from the shack or anywhere else.

While Luke kept an eye on their

surroundings, Brandon followed him over to the wagon. By the time he knelt beside the detective, Luke was opening the bag.

He cursed.

"What is it?"

"They must've transferred the money to their pockets."

"The bag's empty?"

"Not entirely."

Luke reached inside and brought out a cylinder of dynamite.

"My God," Brandon croaked.

Luke was rummaging inside the bag. "Don't fret. This stuff's about as stable as you're likely to get, otherwise Barney Phipps wouldn't have risked lugging it over half these mountains. And what do you know? We've got caps and fuses here, too; everything we need to throw a little dynamite party of our own."

Brandon looked into his sweat-stained face. "You're not thinking of *using* that stuff?"

"If our boys're holed up in that cabin, can you think of a better way to flush 'em out?"

Brandon couldn't. Growing agitated now that their hunt seemed to be reaching its climax, he alternated between watching Luke prepare the explosives and keeping an eye on the silent cabin on the far side of the grassy sward. As Luke finished up, a sound from behind caused them to turn around. A couple of townsmen had light-footed it along the dog-trot and were now watching them with a blend of curiosity and fear. Although they were clutching saddleguns, they made no attempt to use them. Perhaps they'd seen Luke salivate Casey outside the general store, and figured rightly that he was on their side.

The men from the Mountain View turned their attention back to the cabin. With three ready-capped sticks of explosive stuffed into the pockets of his buckskin jacket, Luke went down onto his belly and snaked under the wagon and on through the mostly-dead, trash-littered grass that led closer to the shack. Brandon went after him, a heady brew of anticipation and apprehension chasing off all his fatigue and making him feel a little nauseous.

There was a little swell up ahead that would give them sufficient cover from which to launch their assault. By the time they reached it, the shack was no more than forty feet away.

Flies buzzed erratically through the afternoon heat. Luke ignored them, elbowed up and called out, "Hello, the house!" His voice sounded strange, booming into a silence broken only by the soft, splashing sounds of the river out beyond the structure. "It's all over, Phipps! There's no place left to run, so come on out of there with your hands up!"

There came no response, but both Luke and Brandon could just about detect movement within the old shack.

"I've got some of your dynamite out here, Barney!" Luke called out. "If it'll help to get you fellers out of there, I'll send some in!"

Still there was no response.

"It looks as if they want to do this the hard way, Heller," Brandon whispered.

Luke took one of the nitro-packed sticks from his pocket. "You'd better strike me a match, then," he said grimly.

9

BRANDON fished out a match. He was all fingers and thumbs. At last he scratched the thing to life and Luke held his shaky hand steady long enough to light the dynamite fuse.

Brandon stared at the little flame in morbid fascination as it threw off sparks and ate its way slowly up towards the cap.

Luke's tone was implacable as he shouted out again. "Last chance, Barney!"

There was a movement inside the shack, but no-one sang out and no-one came out.

"For God's sake, Heller," Brandon gasped, his eyes still fixed on the greedy flame. "*Throw* it!"

Luke darted a glance at the fuse, estimating the length of time he had left before the whole thing blew. By his reckoning, he had seconds, maybe ten . . . nine . . . eight . . .

He came up into a low crouch and pulled back his right arm to make the throw.

. . . seven . . . six . . .

If the men who'd killed Jess Monroe thought he was bluffing, they'd soon find out different.

If they were in there, that was.

If . . .

. . . five . . . four . . .

It hit him, then, right out of the blue; that recurring dream of his, about the night the Pinkertons had gone after Jesse James with their 'Grecian fire', the way they'd fire-bombed the Samuels home, killed young Archie and blown Zerelda James' right arm off, all for naught.

. . . three . . .

He knew in that moment that as much as he wanted to get even with the men who'd robbed the Mountain View and murdered the young bell-hop, he could not risk another indiscriminate attack like that one.

He changed aim in the very moment that the shack's old door began to screech open on rusty hinges, and the dynamite flew through the air on a course that took it over towards a scrubby patch of weeds and wild flowers instead of straight at the cabin, and when it detonated, it went with a roar and a flash, and sent a shiver through the ground beneath them as if a giant had just banged his fist against it in anger.

A couple of long seconds ticked away as smoke from the explosion drifted on the air. Then an old, whiskery man stepped out of the battered shack with a brown mongrel dog at his heels. The man was alone apart from the dog. God, thought Luke. *He'd been all alone in that shack, too.*

"Don't shoot! You hear me, whoever you are? I ain't got no money! Ol' Jake ain't got nothin'!" the pitiful figure croaked.

When he started to tap a cane against the ground, it became obvious that he was blind.

Thinking of the near-miss this man had just had — and all because of *him* — Luke shuddered.

Cautiously they broke cover, because it was equally obvious now that the robbers were nowhere in the area. Brandon spoke up. "It's all right, mister. You're safe enough, we mean you no harm . . ."

"Don't shoot me . . ." old Jake repeated. At his side, the mongrel growled menacingly at them.

Luke scanned the backlot in both directions before he could find his voice. "Which way's the ferry, Jake?"

Calling the blind man by his name seemed to calm him down a bit. "The ferry?" he echoed. "North from h-here . . ."

He raised his cane to point — but by then Luke and Brandon were already headed that way, crashing through undergrowth and following an old, weed-choked track through a stand of cypress trees.

Above the din of disturbed blue jays they heard a series of shouts, some angry, some menacing, nothing clear but enough to keep them on the right track.

They came out of the trees no more than thirty yards from the crude wooden pier to which the ferry-boat had been moored just as the robbers were starting to cast off and begin hauling the flat-bottomed, weather-peeled big vessel across the river by means of the thick cables stretching from one shore to the other. Henry Barrow spotted them first, and as he called the alarm, he sent a couple of bullets after them to delay the inevitable confrontation.

Luke and Brandon hit the ground straightaway and rolled to put a tick-infested deadfall between themselves and the men so determined to plug them. Down by the river's edge a thick-armed fellow in a plain cotton shirt and grey pants was coming up onto his knees and holding his head. That was the ferry-man, Luke guessed, and it looked as if Phipps and the others had pistol-whipped him pretty thoroughly to get aboard that packet.

He came up behind the deadfall with the Frontier Colt producing thunder, and beside him Brandon followed his example.

As the ferry began to pull slowly away from the pier, Henry Barrow and Paget set up a fearsome retaliatory fusillade while Barney Phipps, probably the weakest man there, hauled desperately on the quivering cables.

The sound of gunfire was harsh and endless. It was only a matter of time before one side or the other scored a hit. Then, sure enough, Brandon suddenly cried out, came up and went over backwards, and Luke, twisting around to check the damage, voiced an oath — then went very quiet.

There were two holes in the lawyer's chest, and they were both leaking crimson at a shocking rate. Blood was also snaking from Anthony Brandon's nose and mouth.

He did not have long to live. But Luke knew also that unless he did something to check them quickly, the killers would soon be beyond his reach.

There was no way he was going to leave this dying man, though, so he pulled off his kerchief to try plugging the wounds. "Hold still now, Brandon . . ."

Not that Brandon was about to go anywhere, except first into shock, and pretty soon after that, into another, altogether more peaceful place.

"It's . . . it's bad, isn't it?" Brandon asked fearfully.

"I haven't seen much worse," Luke said candidly. "But hold still now and I'll do what I can for you . . ."

The attorney's face twisted up into a mask of despair. He didn't want to die. Who did? But as Luke made to help him, Brandon got a grip on himself, shook his head, reached up and grasped his left hand. "There isn't time for that," he said.

"But — "

"I m-mean it. J-just . . . go get the . . . the men who've killed me, Heller. Settle the account with them . . . for . . . for me and for your f-friend, the bell-boy . . . "

Luke bit down hard. "Oh, I'll get 'em. You can count on that. But . . . listen to me, Brandon. Time's running out. Is there anything you want to tell me before . . . ?"

Brandon forced a smile that quickly turned into a grimace. "A . . . confession, you mean? About whether or not I had anything to do with Austin's . . . murder?" He shook his head. "No, Heller. I'm no angel — yet. But I'm not your man, either. B-but . . . for w-what it's worth . . . "

Brandon gurgled something indistinguishable.

Luke bent closer. "What was that?"

Brandon coughed up some more blood, then repeated what he'd been trying to say before. It didn't take long. There really wasn't much to it. Then the attorney fixed him with a very serious look, although Luke knew he was seeing something, or someone, else, quite literally a lifetime away.

"Tell Juliet . . . goodbye . . . " he husked.

His voice tapered off as life left his bloodied form, and Luke bowed his head still further, worn down by so much senseless death in so short a space of time.

But as he'd reminded himself just after Jess Monroe had died, there was no time to mourn the dead yet, not while the living still had some scores to settle.

His face was a mask as he emptied the Colt and thumbed in fresh loads. His green eyes were flat, cold, hard and determined. He snapped the gate shut and reached for Brandon's .38. He emptied that too, and found reloads in the left-hand pocket of the dead man's sheepskin jacket, along with the rest of the sulphur-head matches.

Luke Heller was going to war.

When he came up and over the deadfall he had a blazing Colt in each fist. He was no longer just a man, he had somehow transformed into something more, an avenging angel, cold, calculating, a little light-headed from lack of sleep, whisker-chinned and travel-stained, but somehow remorseless, unstoppable, inevitable.

He covered open ground at a run, extending one hand, triggering a round, extending the other and doing it all over again, an army of one with blood coursing red-hot through his veins and all considerations but the completion of this one final mission shoved to the back of his mind.

He saw with satisfaction that the ferry hadn't gone far, maybe eighty feet, tops. The current was pushing the craft sideways-on, for one thing; for another, none of the men aboard the vessel knew the first thing about handling it correctly.

Paget threw lead back at him. It

buzzed through the air or threw up little explosions of dust around him. Down by the shore, the ferry-man made to rise, still holding his blood-matted head, but Luke yelled at him to keep down, and still half-dazed and fearful of another beating, he did as he was told without argument.

At last Luke reached the pier, boot-heels clattering against the peeling boards, and threw himself off the southward side, so that all the water-lapped joists and shadows down there would conceal him from the men he was going to nail. At once a flurry of lead ploughed up splinters overhead.

Out in the river, the little ferry-boat had come to a halt as all hands took the opportunity to get Luke off their tail once and for all.

Shoving his Colt away and stuffing the spare into his belt, he took out the second of his three sticks of dynamite and produced a match. His face was a slimy mix of sweat and dust as he waded calf-deep into the water and let loose a roar that was hoarse and choked with fury.

"You men! Listen to me! I'm giving you one last chance to surrender, or so help me I'm gonna blow you out of that water!"

The only response from the boat was another round of shots that sent lead smashing into the pier-posts nearby. Then Phipps and Barrow began struggling to right the vessel and continue pulling it across the river again while Paget hastily reloaded his .45.

Luke smiled grimly. All right. He'd given them a chance, which was a damn'-sight more than they'd given Jess and Brandon. He struck a match against the nearest post. Because the post was damp, he had to scratch it again, once more, before it would light. He touched the tiny yellow flame to the tip of the fuse, let it burn down a little; then, leaning out from the far side of the pier so that he was sheltered from the men in the ferry, he tossed the sputtering stick high into the air.

The explosive charge went end over end, high, higher, highest, graceful as any bird, the fuse dangling from its mouth like a worm spitting sparks as it reached its zenith and began to descend.

It seemed to come down faster than it had gone up, and it went off just as it struck the river's surface, about a dozen feet from the ferry-boat, sending up a great geyser of white water to accompany its gargantuan roar.

The waves set up by the blast knocked the vessel still further off course. Luke watched it slew lazily to one side, knew a fierce, primeval sense of triumph as the robbers fought desperately to maintain their footing on its heaving deck.

He took out the third stick and produced another match. "Give it up, you men!" he bawled. "I mean it!"

He knew they wouldn't, though, and he was already striking the lucifer even as he yelled the ultimatum.

One of the robbers, Barrow maybe,

sent a couple of wild shots after him. But they were in chaos now, all three of them, and when Luke came around the pier's-edge with the third stick of nitro spluttering in his hand, their disorder, their sheer blind panic, was complete.

Luke took quick aim and threw the explosive overarm. On the ferry-boat, the robbers watched it as though transfixed. Then Paget shucked off all pretence at defiance and leapt off the boat and into the water, hoping to put distance between himself and the target the ferry-boat represented.

Barney Phipps was just about to do likewise when the dynamite came down, hit the deck and bounced. Barney's eyes went wide when he saw it, and he froze for vital seconds. Then he scrambled towards the dynamite, snatched it up and made to toss it overboard.

He never made it.

The explosion blew the ferry's stern to splinters and catapulted Barney's suddenly-dismembered form high into the air.

Instinctively Luke flinched as the dynamite went off and the ferry disappeared in a bright amber fireball. Then the sky was raining wreckage, lengths of wood from plank-size to splinters, and the water around the craft appeared to be boiling.

Luke shook his head to clear it. The explosions had left him partially deafened. He turned, waded back through the shallows, up the riverbank, past the stunned ferry-man and onto the pier. He expected to feel jubilation. Instead he felt tired as hell.

The smouldering remains of the boat were turning sluggishly in the current and beginning to rock slowly downriver. Nearby, the man from Tombstone saw a body floating face-up in the blood-clouded water, a shard of wood projecting from its stomach.

It was Henry Barrow.

As he watched, the body slowly capsized and murky water covered those sightless, vaguely surprised eyes. He followed its progress as it drifted on after the ruined ferry, streaming blood to mark its passage.

Then he caught a movement off to his right and turned that way.

"Helle — uh! Heller! For the love'a God — uh! Help *me!*"

Paget was pounding at the water about twenty feet out, sending up a furious white spray all around him. He appeared to be clutching some kind of jute bag in his left hand. His distinctive white-blond hair was flattened across his skull and forehead now, and his face was a grimace. He disappeared beneath the river's restless surface for a moment, then came back up in an explosion of disturbed waves, gasping and screeching and generally looking as good as finished.

Luke stood on the pier watching him for a while. It was only a matter of time before the gunman realised he was almost to shore, and when at length that happened, he dragged himself out of the shallows with his chest heaving, making little moaning sounds as he caught his breath. When he flopped belly-down in among the reeds and grass lining the river's-edge, he was muttering some exhausted-sounding gibberish that might have been a prayer.

Luke came down off the pier and across to him, water squelching in his own boots. Paget was unarmed now, and no threat. Without ceremony he tore the sodden jute bag from the other man's grasp, pulled it open and looked inside. It was as he'd thought; the little bag contained the money the robbers had taken from the Mountain View Hotel.

"All right, mister! No sudden moves, now! We got you covered!"

Luke glanced tiredly over one shoulder. The lard-bellied town constable was coming out of the cypress trees with a .45/70 braced against his shuddering midriff, and behind him was a whole passel of other townsmen, armed with everything from pitchforks to riot guns.

When they saw what had become of the ferry, they slowed down to gawk in disbelief. Luke chose that moment to throw down the jute bag and raise his hands to show that he was going to come quietly.

"All right, constable. Come ahead. Believe it or not, I can explain all of this."

The constable came forward at a trot, his brown eyes shuttling from the smouldering ferry to the body of Henry Barrow, from that to the stunned ferryman, and from him to Paget's heaving form.

"I hope to hell you *can*, mister," the lawman said fervently. "For your sake, I hope to hell you can."

★ ★ ★

Like all these situations, it started out real confused and slowly began to unravel itself. They took Luke down to the jailhouse, and while the Blair Town mortician and his opposite number, the local sawbones, got busy doing what they did best, the man from Tombstone laid it all out plain for the constable.

Afterwards, the lawman locked him in the single strap-steel cell and hustled down to the doctor's surgery to have words with the ferry-man and Paget, then wire the Mountain View Hotel to see what he could do to verify the tale.

Left alone in the jailhouse, Luke pulled off his ruined boots, shrugged out of his buckskin jacket and stretched out on the straw mattress.

He was beat. But judging from the sounds filtering in from the street, Blair Town was still buzzing with news of the recent conflict. Mid-afternoon sunlight shafted in through the barred window above the bunk, clean and golden. It was warm and slightly stuffy in the cell, but Luke was too tired to care much about that.

When he closed his eyes, however, sleep eluded him. All he could see in his mind's eye was Anthony Brandon; Brandon, who'd paid the ultimate price for helping him. And thinking of Brandon made him remember what the attorney had said to him just before he'd died.

He started adding things together then, and damn' if they didn't start making sense.

Eventually he drifted into a deep and dreamless sleep. Although he had no way of knowing it at the time, he would never relive that recurring nightmare of his again.

The next time he awoke it was somewhere around the supper hour, and the constable had brought him over a pail of stew from the cafe across the street.

As Luke dug in, the lawman said, "Your story checks out, Heller. That feller we're holdin' down at Doc Weston's place, Paget, has pretty much confirmed it — not that he could very well do much else, him bein' found with that stolen money an' all, an' with a record as long as your arm to boot. Fix — he's the train conductor you took the gun away from — he's confirmed what you an' that other feller told him when you boarded the train at Haynesville. And I've just had wires back from a feller calls himself Colfax, out at the Mountain View Hotel, an' another from Deb Ward, over to Grey Springs."

"Does that mean I'm free to go?"

"I guess it does. But the money you recovered stays here. Can't just have you walkin' off with that. That'll have to be collected by someone in authority."

"Ward?"

"I know him; he'll do."

Luke ate his fill, then rose up from the bunk. "Anywhere around here I can get a shave and brush-up, constable?"

"I keep my shavin' tack on that shelf under the mirror. Go ahead an' welcome."

"Thanks. When's the next train out of here?"

"By Christ, you're keen to get away, ain't you?"

"Can you blame me?"

"Well, they's a train out at ten in the mornin'."

"Nothing sooner?"

"'Fraid not. But you're welcome to bunk in here for the night, iffen you like."

"I guess I've got no choice. Thanks."

It took a while to quit Blair Town next morning. There were the farmer's horses, Missy and Sampson, to locate and board at Fordyce's Livery, for one thing . . . and there were temporary arrangements to make for Anthony Brandon, until he could find more details about the man's next-of-kin, and where they'd want the body shipped.

Once he got all that out of the way, though, he caught a train out of town and rode the rails back the way he'd come, feeling somehow emptied by Brandon's death and what he thought he'd uncovered about Austin Cameron's murder.

At last the train steamed into Haynesville and after a little asking around he located and paid board for Goddam and Brandon's rented charcoal. What followed was a slow ride back through the pine-scented mountains as the westering sun slid slowly behind the timbered slopes to his back.

It was early evening when he climbed down in front of the stables behind the hotel, and gave the reins over to a livery-boy not much older than Jess Monroe. He stood there in the peaceful dusk, looking up at line upon line of lamp-lit windows, listening to the sounds of the string quartet playing in the dining room. Then he went around the building and up into the reception.

He did not stop at the desk. He went straight upstairs. He had some checking to do. In all it took him twenty minutes.

At last he came back into the reception and told the desk-clerk to send for the Grey Springs sheriff. Then he asked for Mr Colfax.

"Mr Colfax is in the dining room, Mr Heller."

"Send a boy in to fetch him, will you? Tell him I'll be up in room two-seventeen."

The desk clerk nodded. "I'll see to it personally, Mr Heller. I know he's been anxiously awaiting your return."

Luke pushed away and went upstairs. At the second floor he strode down the softly-lit hallway until he came to the door he was after. He pulled in a breath and then tapped a low tattoo on one of the panels. He heard a floorboard creak inside, then Juliet Cameron's soft, breathy voice, asking who was there.

"It's me, ma'am. Luke Heller."

The door opened fast and the beautiful blonde woman was revealed there, stunning in a flowing black velvet gown. Her deep blue eyes travelled from Luke's face to some spot beyond his shoulder. She was hoping to find Brandon there, he knew. Even though the Blair Town constable had wired all the details through to Ward and Colfax, and the dapper little Englishman had almost certainly come to tell her about the attorney's death, she was still hoping to see him there.

As he watched, her anticipation died like a flower in a desert. Steeling herself as best she could, she said, "It . . . It's true, then? A-about about Anthony?"

He nodded. "Yes'm. It's true."

She made no reaction at first. He looked at her, wondering if she'd heard what he said. Then her full lips trembled a little and her eyelids fluttered and the blood drained from her beautiful, beautiful face and he knew that she'd heard him all right.

"Oh God," she whispered.

"Go and sit down, ma'am," he said quietly but firmly, and she did as she was told, in a daze.

He stepped into the room after her. "If it's any consolation," he said gently, "I was proud to ride beside him, Mrs

Cameron. He was a better man than I gave him credit for, and I still feel his death myself."

He heard footsteps on the hallway carpet and turned just as Colfax, his round face still showing the bruises sustained during the robbery, appeared in the doorway. "Mr Heller! I could hardly get up here quick enough when Hollister told me you were back — " His voice trailed off as his own blue eyes shuttled down to the weeping woman seated on the sofa beneath the night-darkened window, and after exchanging a glance with Luke, he hustled across to console her. "My dear Mrs Cameron, please, take heart . . ."

Luke closed the door and watched them for a moment. Then he said, "I know who murdered your husband, Mrs Cameron."

They looked up at him, both of them.

"It was Jess Monroe," he said softly.

Colfax looked at him in disbelief. "*What?* The bell-boy? No, Heller, you're wrong. You *must* be."

"I wish I was, Mr Colfax. But facts are facts. Jess was practically the first man on the scene when Mr Cameron was shot. Near as I could tell at the time, the murder weapon was a small-calibre pistol. When I found Jess laying out there just after Phipps and the rest of them had shot him and then run him down with their horses, he was clutching a Colt Wells Fargo — a .31-calibre handgun."

The Englishman was still frowning. "And you call that evidence?"

"Taken alone, no. But I had his confession, too."

"Confession?"

"Uh-huh. Only I just didn't realise it at the time. You see, just before he died, Jess said, 'I shot 'em. Didn't do me no good, though, did it?' But when we caught up with the robbers, wasn't a one of 'em who'd stopped a bullet. What Jess'd been trying to say was 'I shot *him*.' Your husband, Mrs Cameron."

Colfax still didn't buy it, though. "How do you know the boy wasn't raving, Heller? My God, he was in enough pain. He could have *thought* he'd shot one of those outlaws."

"Sure," Luke agreed. "But I checked through his things when I got back a little while ago, and found something real interesting sneaked away at the bottom of his locker. Seven hundred and fifty dollars." His voice turned hard. "Now, as generous as you are to your staff, Mr Colfax, I don't believe you paid him so well that he could afford to save that much money. Neither do I think he could've stolen it without someone kicking up a fuss."

"Then . . . what is the alternative?" Juliet Cameron asked in a thick shuddery voice.

"Someone paid him to kill your husband, ma'am," Luke replied. "*You*, Mrs Cameron."

The woman came up like a jack-in-the-box, outraged and feisty. "What? This is — "

"I'd as soon you didn't insult me by trying to deny it," Luke cut in. "I've put it all together; *all* of it. Mrs Cameron, you wanted your husband out of the way so that you could try to rekindle the romance you once had with Anthony Brandon — a man so principled that he wouldn't dare entertain the idea of conducting an affair with somebody else's wife, no matter how much she might've meant to him.

"But what was the alternative? To file for divorce might have left you without funds, and I don't believe you wanted to lose out on your husband's money." Luke paused. "Remember the day we first met? You told me your husband was stronger than he looked. Mrs Cameron, I'll just bet he was. You couldn't wait for him to die a natural death — so you hired someone just gullible enough to be taken in by money and, who knows, maybe the promise of something more, and you had him killed."

"That is a disgusting accusation!" the woman spat.

"Oh, I haven't finished yet," Luke replied calmly. "Because you weren't in it alone, were you, Mrs Cameron? There was one other person who wanted your husband dead . . . and that was *you*, Mr Colfax."

"*What?*"

"Brandon was the one who put me onto you," the Tombstone detective replied. "Yours was the name he gave me just before he died. I couldn't understand why at first. So right after I finished taking a look through Jess Monroe's locker, I went and took a look around your office — "

"Now see here — "

" — and then I understood," said Luke.

It went very quiet.

"It's all there, Colfax. That's one thing I *will* say for you; you keep meticulous records. I only spent ten minutes going through your files, but I soon gathered from your correspondence that the Colfax empire's not quite as stable as it looks. In fact, it appears that you've made quite a few bad investments over the last couple of months. Certainly enough to worry the bank that helped you finance *this* place — the bank Austin Cameron represented."

"I will not stand here and listen to this rubbish any longer!" Colfax said sanctimoniously.

"Mr Colfax, you haven't got a choice," Luke replied mildly.

"But the very idea is preposterous!" snarled Colfax. "Why should I want to kill Austin Cameron? His murder has been the worst possible news for this hotel!"

"Now you know as well as I do that *that* is a downright lie. The day you asked me to find Cameron's killer — a nice touch, that, Mr Colfax, made no doubt because Barney Phipps' sudden appearance labelled him as a prime suspect in the case — you told me that five guests had already checked out. But a little while later, whilst I was going through the register on some other business, I couldn't find any evidence that anyone had checked out at all. Still, why should you lie about it?

"The answer was simple, of course. You wanted it to *look* as if Cameron's murder was bad news for the Mountain View. But the truth was very different. You just couldn't lose. If people stopped coming, you'd find a way of claiming compensation on your insurance. On the other hand, a little notoriety wouldn't do the place any harm. In fact, if the enquiries I saw piled up in your secretary's in-tray were anything to go by, I'd say you've already received some mighty lucrative reservations from all kinds of folks back East who want to come and catch a little of that real wild west excitement for themselves."

With a glare in Heller's direction, the dapper Englishman turned to face Juliet Cameron. "My dear lady, I am so sorry that you have had to listen to these scandalous accusations — "

But it wasn't going to wash. "Cameron was here to ask you for more security against your already over-extended credit, wasn't he?" Luke prodded.

Colfax said, "No."

But Juliet said, "Yes."

"Mrs Cameron . . . " the Englishman warned softly.

She looked up at Colfax through dead eyes. "Where is the sense in continuing with this pretence?" she asked in a lifeless voice. "Anthony is dead, and I only did it for him, to win him back."

Luke let his breath out through his teeth. "Let's hear it then, ma'am."

She turned her very blue eyes onto him. "You are right, Mr Heller. About everything. Austin *was* here to ask for a greater stake in the hotel. But not for the bank. For *himself*. In return — "

"Mrs — "

"Let her go on, Colfax."

"In return," the woman said in a sad,

dead voice, "he would stop the bank from restricting John's — Mr Colfax's — credit altogether. Not that the bank had any real intention of doing such a thing unless Austin recommended it, which he was quite willing to do if it helped to pressure John into giving him the stake he desired."

"So you killed him," Luke said quietly. "I can't imagine how the two of you got together and plotted this business in the first place, but the rest of it's easy enough to figure out. You wanted Cameron dead, but you didn't want to do the deed yourselves, so you concocted the phoney attempted-robbery story and somehow talked Jess Monroe into doing it for you." He shook his head sharply, his expression one of contempt. "Christ. He was seventeen years old. Seven hundred and fifty dollars must've looked like all the money in the world to him. And as for the prospect of bedding you, Mrs Cameron? I'll just bet you had him eating out of your hand, didn't you?"

He swallowed hard and pulled the key out of the lock. "Sheriff Ward should be here in a while. Until he arrives, you two can stay in here." He opened the door and went outside, looking back once. "Don't bother to try busting out. There's nowhere to go, for one thing, not a-foot as you two'll be."

Colfax stepped forward, his face like suet in the lamp-glow. "Heller — "

Luke closed and locked the door behind him.

He stood there for a moment, feeling somehow soiled by the crime these people had committed. He wanted to get out of this place, these mountains, and surround himself with folk of his own kind once again.

But first he had to see the sheriff, write up a full statement and sign it before witnesses. Only once that was done, and he had some guarantee that Colfax and the woman would pay for their felony, could he begin to put this business behind him once and for all.

★ ★ ★

He went downstairs and told Hollister, the desk-clerk, to have one of the guides or hunters stand guard on room 217 until he said otherwise.

Hollister, who knew for sure that something was going on and wanted very much to find out what it was, tried to fish a little. "If it's a security matter, Mr Heller, shall I have one of the boys locate Mr Nodeen?"

Nodeen. Luke had almost forgotten about that big lug. "Where *is* Mr Nodeen, anyway?" he asked casually.

"I believe he's ... " Hollister faltered.

"In the bar?"

The desk-clerk cracked a sour smile. "Probably."

"Then let's not disturb him."

"Very good, Mr Heller."

"And have someone fetch me the minute Ward turns up."

"Yes, sir."

That done, he went back upstairs, to

the third floor this time, and Mai.

She damn'-near tore the door off its hinges when he knocked and told her who was there. She pulled him to her and he wrapped her in his arms and kicked the door shut behind him, and after that they spent a good while seeing who could hug the other tightest, until at last they broke apart and he held her at arms-length and they just stood there looking at each other and grinning and feeling foolish and wonderful all at once.

At last the Oriental girl sobered. "Is it true?" she asked. "About this man Brandon?"

His smile also died. "Yeah, it's true."

Silence engulfed them.

With effort he shrugged off the dark mood that threatened to possess him, and gestured to the chest of drawers. "Get your things packed, Mai. We're getting out of here just as soon as I tie up a few loose ends with Sheriff Ward."

A frown creased her delicate oval

face. "Leaving?" she echoed. "But your work here . . . " He said, " — is finished." Then he told her all there was to tell about Cameron's murder.

She came back into his arms toward the end of it, to take and offer comfort against the sickness of it all, and he felt the closeness of her, the heat of her, the smell of her, and wanted to spend the rest of his life in a place where there was no such thing as murder and death, just loving her.

A knock at the door postponed but did not break the moment just then, and when he answered it he found a bell-hop with a prominent Adam's apple standing there, smooth-faced, as yet uncorrupted by the world and its ways.

"Mr Heller? Sorry to disturb you, sir, but Mr Hollister sent me up to tell you the sheriff's just arrived."

Luke nodded. "Thanks, son. Put him in Mr Colfax's office, will you? I'll be down in a minute."

"Sure."

Luke turned back into the room, saw her waiting there for him, waiting to begin easing all the pain from him and he knew a longing that was more spiritual than physical, though it was certainly physical too, and a feeling that was mutual.

"Son," he called out on impulse.

The bell-hop turned back expectantly. "Yes, sir?"

"Make that *five* minutes, will you?"

"Yes, sir."

As the boy continued on his way and Luke closed the door again and went to her in the amber lamp-light, he heard her whisper, "Or ten."

Or what the hell? Fifteen.

THE END

Other titles in the Linford Western Library:

TOP HAND
Wade Everett

The Broken T was big. But no ranch is big enough to let a man hide from himself.

GUN WOLVES OF LOBO BASIN
Lee Floren

The Feud was a blood debt. When Smoke Talbot found the outlaws who gunned down his folks he aimed to nail their hide to the barn door.

SHOTGUN SHARKEY
Marshall Grover

The westbound coach carrying the indomitable Larry and Stretch headed for a shooting showdown.

FIGHTING RAMROD
Charles N. Heckelmann

Most men would have cut their losses, but Frazer counted the bullets in his guns and said he'd soak the range in blood before he'd give up another inch of what was his.

LONE GUN
Eric Allen

Smoke Blackbird had been away too long. The Lequires had seized the Blackbird farm, forcing the Indians and settlers off, and no one seemed willing to fight! He had to fight alone.

THE THIRD RIDER
Barry Cord

Mel Rawlins wasn't going to let anything stand in his way. His father was murdered, his two brothers gone. Now Mel rode for vengeance.